Praise for the *Unthinkable Thoughts of Jacob Green*, an ALA Notable Book and B&N Discover GNW Selection for 2004

"I read it compulsively, rooting every step of the way for its flawed and fractious characters."

—Wally Lamb, author of *She's Comes Undone*

"A funny, heart-twisting story . . . Wry humor, assured prose and a keen sensitivity to the emotional minefields of familial relationships . . . Braff deftly captures the monumental and miniscule moments of everyday life."

—*USA Today*

"Funny and wistful."

—*San Francisco Chronicle*

"Scarifyingly funny debut . . . Painfully honest and surprisingly compassionate . . . Compulsively readable."

—*Kirkus Reviews*

"A rich, moving, and very funny first novel."

—*Booklist* (starred review), Top 10 First Novel of 2004

"Josh uses meticulously drawn scenes of childhood antics to give his novel its almost effortless momentum."

—*The Forward*

"Hilarious and achingly sad in its depiction of a teenage boy's troubled family."

—*The Oakland Tribune*

"Jacob Green has a lot of 'unthinkable thoughts' — and Braff's great ear and lively voice communicate them with plenty of laughs and poignancy."

—*The Hartford Courant*

Praise for *Peep Show*

"Braff skillfully illuminates the failures and charms of a broken family. That teen longing for adults to act their age haunts long after the final page." — *People Magazine* (4 stars)

"Whether he's writing about religion, pornography, or the family ruined by both in this smart, funny, heartbreaking novel, Braff does it with authority, wit, and an unflagging compassion for his hopelessly broken characters." — Jonathan Tropper, author of *This Is Where I Leave You*

"An interfamilial culture clash of epic proportions. . . . This is a powerful, sensitively told coming-of-age story about the ways in which rigid worldviews extract their pounds of flesh from us all, especially the young." — *Booklist* (starred review)

"An accomplished, thematically complex, but ultimately very relatable piece of writing, a book that convinces us of Braff's talent and ingenuity. . . . disarmingly fresh." — *Spectrum Culture*

"Braff brings together two very different cultures with sympathy for both. . . . An intriguing contrast in the struggle to uphold a set of values and the painful necessity of compromise." — *Publishers Weekly*

"Braff draws an interesting parallel between the peep show aspect of David's father's theater to the screen drawn across his mother's Hasidic world." — *Jewish Book Council*

THE
DADDY
DIARIES

Other books by Joshua Braff

The Unthinkable Thoughts of Jacob Green

Peep Show

THE
DADDY
DIARIES

a novel by

JOSHUA BRAFF

PRINCE STREET PRESS

2015

Published by
Prince Street Press
Lafayette, CA 94549

This is a work of fiction. While, as in all fiction, the literary perceptions and insights are based on experience, all names, characters, places, and incidents are either products of the author's imagination or are used fictitiously. No reference to any real person is intended or should be inferred.

Published in the United States of America by Prince Street Press.

Cover design by David Walker
Interior design by Mauna Eichner and Lee Fukui

ISBN 978-0-9864175-0-4

First edition.

FOR MY WIFE

All we really need is each other,
and the time is always now.

—William Nelson

PART ONE

San Francisco on the Mind

MONDAY | *Lightning*

S
o many years in the pattern of forever. But we break the pact. Say good-bye to close friends and journey off to the flatlands of Tampa Bay, where alligators wade in swimming pools and squirrels stay in trees until the ground stops moving. They call our new home Lightning Alley. My daughter is currently counting the seconds between the flash and roar. "That one was ten," she says, having never seen lighting in all her nine years. Earthquakes, yes. Random bolts of massive electricity, no. I sit up in bed and see one out the window. There is no beginning or warning. It just appears, its shape an abstract bolt, very near the ground. They say keep off the phone, the computer. Twenty-six deaths between 1990 and 2003. My daughter Tara stands at the window, counting the seconds. ". . . three, four, five, six," and we hear the thunder. She looks at me as if the world is no longer a predictable place. "Oh no," she says.

"What?"

"We forgot the charity thing," she says.

I shake my wife awake. "We forgot the bake sale."

3

"Bake sale?"

There must be eleven unused drawers in this new kitchen. I have to concentrate to remember where the spatulas are. As of Friday there were boxes still blocking the pantry door. I kneel before the refrigerator.

"Chocolate chip," Tara says.

Boom! Thunder rattles the windows.

We all look at each other, to see if we're all still here.

"I only see sugar cookies," I say.

"Check the lettuce drawer," my wife says sleepily.

I see them. Cookie sheet, butter. A preheated oven.

"Make a hundred," Tara says.

"Twenty," my wife says. "Only twenty."

"It's for charity, Mom."

"But I only bought enough for twenty."

My son, Alex, enters the kitchen in pajama bottoms only, rustling his hair. He walks to the pantry and sighs deeply. "We're out of Honey Nut Cheerios," he says. "What am I supposed to eat for . . . ?"

"Have Grape-Nuts," my wife, Jackie, says.

"They're gross."

"Waffles?"

He heads for the freezer.

"Good morning, Alex," I say to him. "How'd you sleep?"

"I didn't," he says.

Almost a teen. The move from San Francisco hit him the hardest. My mother's a psychologist. She says leaving the first friends you made in life can be traumatic. She reminds me that I was depressed a lot in high school. That I should watch out for him.

"The cookies are starting to puff up," Tara says, kneeling before the oven window. "Ooh, I can smell them too."

"Terrific," Alex says. "Can't find the syrup."

"The fridge," my wife says.

He finds it and stomps off to his room.

"I don't think he's sleeping at all," Jackie says. "You see his eyes?" The choice to move was a parental one. And financial. There's definitely sacrifice in prioritization. Our move was calculated, researched, had logistical links to our children's education, our livelihood, and the notion of keeping our marital chemistry on its toes. Fifteen years ago we left New Jersey for Northern California and the quaint yet bustling neighborhood near Haight Street known as Cole Valley. I believe San Francisco emits a high-pitched beam of inaudible sound. Only those who live there can hear it. The sound is a message that states we are a religion of region and there are only two laws: (1) connectivity: *you must respect strangers as if they're brothers and sisters*; (2) kindness: *no room for assholes*. The sky there holds little interest in season or prediction. Summer can be rainy, autumn can be ideal. Until the recession arrived I saw the sky as the one I'd grow old under. An old man in a familiar town. In a period of three months I lost one job writing radio ads for KGT. After that it was the tourist brochures I wrote for a local conglomerate in Berkeley. Out of money. They said they'd call when things picked up. In a month my only income became editing college essays and graduate-level theses. My wife Jackie was the CEO of a company that simply lost its backing but didn't mention it to her until the ship was long sunk. I got my teaching resume together and went on a few interviews. And then we hit the jackpot. I remember the moment, during *60 Minutes*. "St. Pete wants me," she said, reading her email.

"St. Petersburg?" I said. "Florida?"

She was silent. I faced her, her eyes lit by her phone. "Might be perfect," she says.

Might be.

"Time to go, kids!" I yell. I carry the twenty cookies to the car, kiss my wife, and we're off to school in a lighting storm. Our street, Appian Way, is already pooling with rain. Our new neighbors call it the Appian River when the rain turns the road into a body of water. It could happen today.

"Daddy, I can't carry all of these cookies from the parking lot. Park near my class, okay?"

The school is private so the rules regarding drop-off and pickup are complicated. How you enter and exit changes when it rains, shines, hits a hundred degrees or drops below sixty. We inch in, people honking already. I park in an area called the "no zone" so I can get Tara close enough to her classroom.

Honk, honk! The moms here are vicious.

"Excuse me!" I hear. "Excuse me, sir." I don't see her yet. But this has happened to me ten times since we started here.

"You cannot park in the no zone," she shouts from her SUV. "You can't park there. Look what you're creating."

"One second," I call out. "My daughter has to carry these cookies so I just did it today."

The woman shakes her head as her tinted window rises.

Honk!

"Honking Nazi."

"This stinks," Alex says. "Let me out of this car."

"Wait," I say, "I'll drive you around to your building."

He jumps out and walks off, hopping his backpack higher. I watch him go, his jaw grinding with frustration.

"Bye, Daddy," says Tara.

"Bye, baby. Careful with the cookies. I'll see you at three sharp in the pickup zone."

Another SUV pulls up to me and stops. I wait for her window to drop. It's Ginger's mom; we met at orientation. Tara and Ginger are friends. Her name is Teri. She is gorgeous, as many Floridian blondes are. Mirrored cop glasses, a yoga tank top, and platinum hair.

"Hi," she says and smiles. "My daughter has brownies for the bake sale. Can I park in your spot so she can walk to class?"

"Of course. I'll pull out, no problem."

I wave to the mom as I leave. My first Florida friend. Someone too pretty to hang out with alone. I follow the driveway around the school. Many of the kids stand outside for the Pledge of Allegiance, read by a student through the intercom. And I see him. Alex. Walking across the football field, alone. I try to park but there's nowhere to pull over. I slow down and get honked at. No zones everywhere. I drive toward the exit and put my car in the teachers' lot. Is he going to class? Phys ed? I walk to the back of the school, to the football field. I don't see him. Against the fence I squint for him. I call my wife and get her voice mail.

"Hi, I just wanted to say . . . hi," I say. "Kids are good. See you later."

Back in my car I decide to drive around one more time. At the football field I see a group of kids. Too far to see if he's one of them. But of course he is. It must be his class.

Sea Level

Today I have long and tedious conversations with people who represent water, gas, pool, cable, alarm, landscape, garbage, neighborhood watch, and insect control, as well as a woman across the street in her nineties who tells me our street floods twice a year.

"We're below sea level," she says, raising one eyebrow. "Do you have sandbags?"

"No."

"How about a kayak?"

Alone in the new house I make the bed and sit, listening to the quiet. I take out my notebook to write. The cover says #79, and beneath that is a bad sketch of my wife. I put her in a Viking helmet. No reason. On a new page I write in caps, ALEX and TARA. I close the book and get in my car. I just start to drive and soon I'm headed for the beach. Ten minutes on the highway and I arrive at Pass-a-Grille, a tiny beach town. Standing on the sand I stare, absorbing the sky that will hover over us indefinitely. I can see the moon, distanced and faded in the clear sky. I'm comforted. Same moon.

Same earth. I take out my notebook again and read the words, ALEX and TARA. Same moon, same earth.

The views here on the west coast of Florida are filled with optimism. Tropical with hundreds of greens and blues, a sunny-happy glow well into the early evening, and always lush with the smell of vacation. The view belongs to everyone here, without cost. I can stare at the sky, the horizon, for long stretches, trying to absorb the wordless message, the obvious lesson in all this blossomed natural color. So many seabirds. Pelicans rule down here. They are large and wise and glide with class. Something in their carriage suggests they know they're indeed living better lives than the robotic humans below them. Surely it's the species that have been here the longest that use their days most productively. Pelicans have eyes like humans, wet and blinking, even pensive, telling me all the stories of the sea. One is very close to me, highly unimpressed. I take his picture. He seems to pose, a widening beak. I laugh to myself. What is it you have to tell me, bird? My thing is insight, I tell him. What's yours? Tell me, through the membrane of your shovel beak, just how I'm supposed to live my life most fully. I know you have a message. It may or may not be for me. Perhaps your story is in the flying, the soaring, the whole getting-to-a-skimming-level, just over the water, taunting us with all we can't be.

I'm just a pelican. Don't overthink it.

No, no, you've been around forever. You must have wisdom, some lesson as to why and what we're doing here on earth. Is it only about learning to forgive and love others?

How the hell do I know? All I think about is eating, shitting, and eating more.

That's so disappointing.

Oh, I see. You're glorifying my life because you see me flying and diving for fish during sunset. You don't think I'd like to see a movie, have a steak with a cloth napkin, get invited to a Super Bowl party? All we get is humans pointing at us, dreaming up stories about our majesty. I eat the same shit every single day.

I've picked a very cranky and disenchanted pelican.

As I leave, I see another seabird drop from the sky and plunge into the ocean with an explosion of splash and wings. He rises and flaps hard with the fish in his mouth, slowly lifting as water pours off his body. Up and off, veering right. And he is gone.

What's a Threesome?

Alex's first birthday in Florida. Thirteen. Getting him to talk or smile these days is tricky. My wife says he's acting normal, for a guy who misses his friends. He's also got some acne, hates the new school and all its rules. Puberty is on him, cramming its heel into every step he takes. I ask him about his classes, new friends, like-minded boys in class, and he says there's one kid from New York who brags about all the "babes" he's "boned." I remember being my son, resembling him. No cash, big sneakers, zero authority, and an achy yet subtle pain beneath each nipple, known as "nipple rock." Poor guy is just arriving, dragged stumbling but steadily into the grip of it all. Half little boy, half werewolf, he's currently most thrown by homework, pop quizzes, the need to stay awake in class, and the distance between himself and his California friends.

Today I pick him up and he has a question. He asks me if the verb *to bang* is the same as *to bone*.

"My guess is that they're the same."

He nods before looking out the window. "What's humping?"

I remember its arrival, sexuality. The symbol of the woman outside bathrooms held new meaning, the forbidden pink beyond her doors. At the mall with my mom in suburban New Jersey, the female mannequins in Bloomingdale's taunted me. Brunettes and strawberry blondes, vixens all, pouting and pointing, lost in their urbane and frozen cocktail stares. Then it was magazines. My brother Cam had a pile under his bed. He showed me where they sold them, in the back of the 7-Eleven. *Penthouse,* the 1979 Playmate of the Year just sitting there on the rack. Raquel Welch as a statuesque cavewoman, wearing an animal-skin bikini made of rabbit, or was it bear? I snuck back to the magazine aisle, nervous, looking back at the clerk, his back turned. So verboten. I flipped quickly through but saw no nudity, just ads, the Marlboro Man, a cartoon boob. My kingdom for the sight of Raquel's right hip. And then I saw them. Both hips. All of her. My very first love.

My son's first love is Coca-Cola. If I'm not around he'll drink three like a longshoreman with a flask. It's something we both like so we bond over it, seek it out in bottle form and in those tiny cans. We enjoy the Americana of the old tin signs, the ubiquity of that reddest of reds, no matter where you go. Tuesday we found Mexican Coke—more syrup, they say, and always in recycled bottles, a connoisseur's favorite. We drank them on our porch.

"Dad?"

"Hmm?"

"Steven Hurley is the kid we met in the school office last week."

"Okay, seemed like a good guy."

"He says sperm whales are called that because they have two tons of sperm inside their whale balls."

"Uh, *baaa,* thanks for playing. Steven is wrong. That's not true."

My son nodded and blinked a lot. "I thought so."

"Sounds like old Steven needs to Google sperm whales," I said.

"He also said the earth will explode soon because of global warming."

"No. Still no. The earth is fine."

"But it could blow up. Just not while we're alive."

"Yes, maybe, but who cares, right? We won't be here."

"But someone will," he said and looked down at his shoelaces.

I rested my hand on his back. "No fears, little man. You are safe forever, okay?"

He looked at me but then returned to his brain, and all its fears. Did I make him pensive? Or is it his mother's intellect? Children bring remarkable perspective. You have to raise them well to tap the code. They have to love you to help you. Or is the word *teach?* I absorb his thoughts, place myself among the questions in his mind. I was him. He'll be me.

Two mornings ago he runs into my bathroom while I'm in the shower.

"I have a pube!"

"You have a what?" I said.

"Look!" He opened the shower door and lowered his pants, keeping his T-shirt lifted with his teeth.

"See it?" he mumbled.

I did, by God. The ending of youth? The beginning of sexuality? The first sign of manhood? Or just a tiny brown hair on my little boy's schmeckel?

"See it, Dad?"

"Yup. I do, I see it there. Congrats, buddy. It's the real thing."

"Mom!" he yelled, and off he went to show her his manhood, without a speck of inhibition. Not the way I remember it. I guess

my parents were raised to keep sexuality deep in the annals of "live
and learn." The Internet wouldn't bloom for decades the day I saw
my first pube. Dr. Ruth hadn't even said "ejaculate" on TV. I do
have a memory of a book called "*Where Did I Come From?*" See
the wiggly guys in top hats? They come rocketing out of your ure-
thra and smash into these little ladies here, the eggs in the yellow
bonnets. Only one gets through. And it could be you.

"Yippee!" I heard my wife yell from upstairs. "Awesome. I *do*
see it." Some applause.

We were just so happy he was talking to us. Finally. The return of Alex. I was so proud of our immunity to the obvious pitfalls
parents face with preteens. I was empowered by the rhythm we'd
finally earned.

And then it pummeled him. Overnight it got worse; a hurricane of hormonal shrapnel came chomping at his bone growth
and left him pimply and sinister. Life blows, he says. I annoy
him. His mother's so lame. My jaw pops when I chew. I only get
a friendly tone or word when I buy him Cokes and he snags them
from my hand like an irritated baby gorilla.

He's depressed, maybe, angry at his circumstances. Perhaps
the school really sucks. I miss him. I think of days not so long ago
when I was his hero, his anchor. I will never be as big to him, as
important, as needed. Puberty will beg him to dismiss me. Will I
ever lift him again, over my shoulder, leaving him giggling just
by kissing and squeezing his soft frame, lost in the embrace of my
good fortune? Being a dad. With my only son.

"Steven also told me what an orgasm is," he says, his forehead
creased with concern. "He says it looks likes mayonnaise."

My mother suggests a book. Not that book. Some book. We'll
give it to him, maybe just leave it in his room, in the bathroom,

near his shoes. I buy one for myself, the latest hit, *Talking to Him: A Father's Guide to His Son's Questions about Sex.*

Page 3: *You are not your son's pal, buddy, or hombre. You may think you are, but you're really not. You're his dad. Will it feel like you're old chums at times? Of course it will. But you are not his friend. He needs you in a different way.*

I find my son in the den. I sit next to him with my new book and watch him play his video game.

"You winning?" I ask, and watch him fire a grenade launcher into a war-torn village.

"Not really."

"Is anyone winning?"

"Dad?"

"Yes?"

"I have a question," he says, his headphones muting the explosions on the screen.

"Okay."

"What's a dirty Sanchez?"

"I don't know."

"What do you mean?" he says, pausing the game, facing me.

"I mean I don't know. A 'dirty Sanchez'?"

"And what's head?"

Head. Great. How do I explain this? I flip to the back of my new book as if the explanation is there.

"I saw it on the wall in the bathroom," he says, returning to his game. "At the restaurant last night. It said, 'Want good head?' and had a phone number."

"Right."

"Is it a drug?"

"No. No, head is just . . . head is slang for a . . . sex thing."

"Intercourse?"

"No. It's slang. There's slang for all different types of words."

"What's a reverse cowgirl?"

I slowly close my brand-new book.

"What's a Ben Franklin?" he says.

I'm lost. I mean below-the-hips-in-quicksand lost. I smile at him and wonder what a "Ben Franklin" could possibly be. I envision a naked colonial man in his sixties with black kneesocks and a kite.

"Will you pause the game?" I ask.

"Why?" he says, repeatedly hitting the "fire" button with the flash of his thumb.

"I think we should talk."

He's willing to walk into his room to speak, so his younger sister doesn't hear us and go blind with shock. In our conversation I learn that my son has not kissed a girl but likes a person named Hannah in social studies. We both learn what constitutes a dirty Sanchez from Google. Whole lot worse than I thought. After we absorb the definition in our own silent ways, we talk about how different people make different decisions when it comes to their own personal sexual lives. We're getting along wonderfully, like old war buddies. Not his friend, my ass!

"You and Mom have only banged twice, right?"

Yikes. Banged. Two times, two babies; I see his math. As I ponder the question he begins to blush. Or is it me? He isn't sure if his query is legal, his eyes soft, already apologetic.

"We've . . . been together . . . more than twice," I say.

He thinks about this for a while. "Nick Adams said his older brother gave his girlfriend a tuna melt."

"I don't know what that is," I say.

"You sure?"

"Yes, I'm sure. Should we Google it?"

"Maxi pad?" he throws out.

"Uh, those are used for . . . menstruation."

He looks down into his lap. "Can I have a Coke?"

We drive to the 7-Eleven. They have Mexican Cokes so I grab a couple before finding my son staring at the *Penthouse* rack near the cash register. He stands close but not too close, and then looks at me but can't see my face through the partition. He approaches the rack and suddenly I'm watching myself in 1979, stealthy, driven, a gnat to a bulb. He places his hand on a magazine.

"Hey kid!" snaps the clerk. "You can't look at that! Got to be eighteen."

"I wasn't!" he says, humiliated, scooting away, hoping I didn't hear.

"Sorry," the clerk says with kindness. "Just the rules."

As I move toward them I see my boy drooping near the exit, a scolded dog. I want to rescue him, erase his angst, lift him from all that he'll endure in this phase of his life.

"Two in the bottle," I tell the clerk, and look down at the *Penthouse*.

Three buxom brunettes, arm in arm, wearing blow-up seahorses around their waists. The caption reads: *Oiling Up for Summer, a Threesome in Maui*. I lift it quickly, proudly, and flip to the core of it, the centerfold. I open the flap and hold it up for my son.

"Look," I say. "No big secret."

"Dad!" he screams in a whisper, a dip in his knees.

I close it fast and place it back on the rack. The clerk and I have eye contact.

My son runs from the store, the doors swinging. I feel so stupid. I embarrassed him at his most vulnerable. I think of the book I bought. "You are not your son's pal, buddy, or hombre. You may think you are, but you're really not. You're his dad."

Inside the car he is ready. "Why would you do that to me?" he says.

"It was stupid. I apologize."

"You opened it. With the guy right there."

"I didn't think. I was only thinking of me. Look," I say, holding the Cokes out to him. "In a bottle. Take one. It's yours. I'm sorry. I'm sorry I did that."

His face softens, his eyes pleased. I pop the cap for him and he takes a long sip. "Yum. The Mexican kind," he says. "I love you, Dad."

Tears rise, a burning beneath my cheeks. I'm so touched, so lonely for his need for me.

"I love you too," I tell him, and bury a kiss into the sweaty brown hair above his ear.

"Dad?"

"Yes?"

"What's a threesome? It said 'A Threesome in Maui' on the magazine."

I find myself sighing as I pull the car out of the lot. "I don't know that one, hombre. I just don't know."

Baby Please Don't Go

| *Overcast with splotches of blue*

My wife's mother is gone. Last year she succumbed after four full years of illness. In hindsight the story that matters is how long she lived after her diagnosis. Alex and Tara were very close with her so the lessons in loss were fast and unforgiving. My mother-in-law's aura was magic, heady, almost visible. I see her in my wife's eyes, and the soft skin of her arms. I see her when I read the *New York Times*, see funny movies, or hear a certain laugh of my daughter's that can only be Nana's. Discussing her life as a family helped us all heal. But after she was gone, I longed for something I hadn't realized I'd had. She helped me become a more complete listener, sympathizer, parent to young kids.

It's been a year now, so we all fly up to New Jersey to see the plaque at her funeral site, a bronze rectangle with her name and birthday on it. My father-in-law chose to keep it just us, asking his friends and even his brothers to let the immediate family gather in private. My mother and stepdad, Roger, are here. We all wear black on a gray day and I wish I'd thought to suggest casual clothes. The vibe is so morbid. We should celebrate her. I watch my father-in-law approach the grave. We all stand in silence and I look at my mother. I can see her mind reeling, perhaps envisioning us all gathering here for her one day. Birth and death, death and mourning. I could use a drink. My father-in-law's shoulders begin to shake. He is crying.

"You took my best smiles with you," he says to the ground, and a frightful sound leaps from my mother's mouth. His words hit her in the jaw, knock the wind out of her. My wife hugs her and my son looks at me, his eyes filled with loss. We did all this last year when she passed. I thought this time would be easier. We should have come in shorts and T-shirts. My father-in-law tries to brighten the mood.

"But I have so much to make me smile," he says. "Just look, just look at all the love I still have."

My daughter swipes at her eyes.

"So don't worry," he says, pointing at us. "I'm covered."

My wife approaches the grave and hugs her father. My daughter rests her forehead on her mom's back and I put my arm around Alex. His reluctance toward me is for all to see. But here, with his emotions stripped down, his cheek rests on my lapel. I remember my little boy, a newborn, and how my mother-in-law was standing outside the delivery room. And how we hugged, and she told me she loved me for the first time. The woman beneath our feet.

"Let's go home," my father-in-law says. "Let's go."

My wife steps away and I hold her close, the emptying of so much emotion.

"I miss her," she says.

"I do too," I tell her.

We all take another long look at the plaque in the grass. Good-bye.

The walk back to the lot is tricky in heels. My wife takes my elbow and I see her foot twist and lie flat, sideways against the ground. She winces and I try to lift her, pulling her elbow. "You're hurting me!" she yells. "Just let me walk on my own!" She takes the shoes off and jogs the rest of the way. She gets in her father's car and slams the door. Everyone is looking at me.

"I was trying to help her," I say.

My mother says, "Helping her sometimes means letting her be."

Great. I walk to the lot and open the door. My wife is rubbing her ankle, her back to me.

"Sorry," she says, sniffing. "Guess I'm not myself today."

"I think we should've worn T-shirts," I tell her.

She faces me, her makeup smeared. "Can we go home now?"

⚡ ⚡ ⚡

Our flight isn't until tomorrow. We settle into my father-in-law's house and the night is stagnant, joyless, it has to be. Even when I'm out of the black suit the air is stale with loss. My father died on a Tuesday when I was six. I didn't go to the funeral but I must've dreamed I was there. My brother Cam was a teenager. He told me they buried our father holding a lock of hair from each of the women he loved in his life. His hand was so covered it looked like Sasquatch. The idea of humor at a funeral works for me. I want people to laugh at mine.

I suggest we watch videos of my mother-in-law and it ends up happening. The footage is of my daughter's first birthday. We're all there, younger, milling about, treating our baby like the princess she is. My mother-in-law has the camera and it shakes a lot, a bit nauseating. But it's funny, so her. She points the thing on herself and speaks.

"Our baby girl is one year old today. She has her whole family here. Say hi," she says, and points the camera at me, my mom, who has much shorter hair, and my wife. We all say "happy birthday" in unison and it scares our daughter to tears. The scene ends with the camera being fumbled but caught again.

I see my father-in-law grinning as he watches his wife, wiping both cheeks.

In bed that night I get a nudge. My wife snuggles closer. "She once told me she wished she had more children."

"Your mom?"

"Yes."

"Did she try to have more?"

"I think so. But I'm not sure."

I reach for her hand. "Think you can sleep?"

"I think we should try."

Yes. Try to live as long as we can. Try to see that life is fleeting. Try to absorb and convey carpe diem for the sake of our children.

"One more baby," she says.

I close my eyes and can almost smell Handi Wipes. What about the violent contractions, the potty training, the drooling, that soft and mushy skull hole on the cranium? The Cheerios everywhere? The fact that Jackie is forty?

"I feel like someone's missing from our dinner table," she says.

My father-in-law's nine-year-old terrier is bumping our door with his paw. I get up and let him in. He walks under the bed and sighs.

"I know you heard me," my wife says.

"Yes. Let's talk about it in the morning," I say.

"Okay."

We are silent for ten minutes at least. And I hear my wife.

"Let's just try."

Trying

Monday. We try. Weird to do it knowing the orgasm might have our kid in it. I care about this batch of semen as if it were my own. Afterward we look at each other and my wife's already glowing. Her eyes suggest we just made a human being, done, way to go, let's pick a name and head off for diapers.

Tuesday. We try twice. I wake up ready, if you know what I mean, and that's number one. I think about Sunday's orgasm and feel a little bad. I'm bringing so many more candidates to the table. We do it again that night, after the kids are asleep. We haven't done it twice in one day since our last vacation. The hotel played *Iron Man* on a blow-up screen near the pool and the kids were gone for two hours. It seems the plan is to bombard my wife's eggs with team after team of baby matter.

Wednesday. I'm really on fire. This may be my best performance since we ventured into this. It's all the practice. A sweat ball falls from my forehead onto my wife's chin. Even this is erotic at the moment. I've never felt more connected to anyone in my life. I see her as the girl I met so young in college. And then I see her as the woman I married. The woman who gave birth to my children. The only woman in the world for me. The fit of our pelvises is absurd, as if the math of our union had been done before we met. I think of serendipity and alchemy and when it's over we lie like prizefighters, my arm draped over her lower back.

Thursday. In the midst of trying I have a thought. Our kids were easy to conceive. We were so lucky. It'll probably be fast again. Mathematically it's hard to deduce the exact night my son was conceived. My wife says it was in a B&B in Half Moon Bay. We think our girl was built on a boring night at home. My wife, currently on top of me, asks me what I'm thinking about. I shake my head to indicate I'm thinking of nothing but thrusting. When we're done I think I've pulled something in my middle back. I get on the floor and stretch it out. She says, "Sorry," and I wonder if she means for putting me in traction.

Friday. In the morning I'm ready again. My wife is asleep. I test my hips by pumping them twice to see if I might be paralyzed during sex. I decide it will hurt. I let her sleep. I feel old.

Saturday. Notebook #79 has a full page of chores I've written down. The orthodontist, Tuesday at three thirty. Eye doctor (new school requirement). They both need all their paperwork in for registration. Call Dr. Farning in San Francisco and have medical forms sent to school. Vinyl lining under the roof overhanging the driveway is drooping. Possible rodent issue, as they climb ivy to get in gutters. Call Marcus the handyman. The pool filter is whistling more than humming. Call Cyril the pool man, phone number on fridge. Get stamps. Mail unstamped envelopes on kitchen counter. Sheets on guest bed, old and thinning, ripped in one spot. Mom arrives on the fifth. Back of freezer has a yellowing ice buildup. May be leak in pantry, look for dark spot on ceiling in corner where we keep cereal. Call your brother in New York.

Monday. Been a while, enjoying it tremendously. How did I end up with such a sexy woman? Oh baby. We're making a baby.

Tuesday. Before we start, I ask my wife if she'd mind approaching me slowly, in a "seductive way." She's not sure what I mean but tries. She does a halfhearted Mae West walk. Who cares. We got a job to do.

Thursday. In the garage. I don't know, just a change of environment. It's not a great floor so we do it standing. During intercourse I take a look around. I cannot believe my leaf blower's been in here the whole time. I spent a year and a day looking for it during our last rainstorm. There's no air-conditioning in here. We're baby making in a sweatbox. If I keep this up I'm going to lose fifteen pounds. My phone is ringing in my pants. Where are my pants? I see them. In a ball near my leaf blower.

"I better get it," I say.

"Can you finish?"

I stare at her back, the skin, a birthmark I've known since the early nineties. I love you, thank you for loving me.

"It's the school," I say, checking the message afterward.

My daughter is in the infirmary. She wants me to come pick her up because she got hit with a dodgeball. I have the nurse put her on the phone.

"Hello?" she says.

"What happened, sweetie?"

"Stupid Matt Wilson happened. He threw the ball at my stomach and now I feel like I'm going to throw up."

"Can you wait a few minutes and see how it feels?"

Silence.

"Do you want me to come get you?"

"Uh-huh."

"But it's so early. What are you gonna do at home all day?"

"I don't know. Watch movies?"

"Put your hand on your stomach," I say.

"Okay."

"Now rub it slowly and see if it helps?"

Silence.

"Are you doing it?"

"No. Will you get in the car and come get me now?"

Silence.

"I'll be right there."

Business Trip

Househusband is a relatively new term to Americans. If I'd heard it before I became one, I'd probably have agreed that the two words together could only connote laziness. One longtime colleague of my wife's heard about my life in Florida and said, "It's like he's in high school but without all the bullshit." I absorbed his words carefully, asking myself if he was right. He's a nice person, doesn't have kids, eats out every night, and has never once made a school lunch, cooked SpongeBob mac and cheese, or convinced a little girl that her closet is empty of nocturnal ghouls. He's never dressed as a pilgrim, utilized the back burners on his stove, wrestled a roll of Saran Wrap for twelve long minutes, cleaned out a thermos of chili, or clipped toenails during *The Voice*. I wonder if he's stepped on Legos, tied little shoes, packed backpacks, washed socks, or followed trails of Nutella smears or crushed Froot Loops, Cheddar Bunnies or Goldfish? Has this colleague who compared me to a high school student ever dillydallied in bedtime cuddling, tiny teeth brushing, ponytail construction, ear-pierce cleaning, or calling the mother of a child's classmate to set up a playdate?

I wonder if he'd keep calling it a playdate, even if his daughter made it clear that it was now referred to as a "get together."

The wife is away, four nights this time, a huge video gaming convention in Los Angeles. Depending on the morale level after Mom is wheels-up, we either eat fun food, buy supermarket toys, or watch borderline inappropriate movies like *The Jerk* and *Caddyshack*. I do fewer dishes, watch late-night TV, and end up in different beds throughout the house. My daughter sleeps in her mother's spot, always mentioning the "smell of her," the leftover DNA. Unlike when she's here, I feed the kids first and nibble my way to midnight. Day one is fine after they understand that Mom's not here until Saturday at 11:00 p.m. I watch them calculate the days in these moments, especially my daughter, who is feeling the agony of each minute without her. The second she realizes there's not a lot she can do about it, she acts normal, all the way to her mother's arrival.

I keep my own loneliness private. I think about drinking alcohol at lunch. I consider clicking on Spankwire.com in order to be sexual . . . alone. I sleep with my socks on. Day three I'm not in a very good mood. I might be sick, or sad. I tell myself it's because it's hard to be a single parent, even if the kids are older, more independent than toddlers but still so very needy. Do I resent her? Is that it? I'm here, home, snoring with my mouth wide and she's in LA having meetings with rich people who smell like scented candles and the wasabi they got on their sleeve at lunch. I should take some copywriter jobs, use the downtime for my own work. I open #79 and write, *Get work in FLA*. The phone rings and I won't pick it up. It rings and rings and the robot lady on the machine announces the caller: "Call from Nee-Yo-Been-So."

I try to figure out who Nee-Yo-Been-So could be.

"Call from Nee-Yo-Been-So."

I glare at the phone, hating Nee-Yo-Been-So in my bone marrow. The second it stops ringing it starts again.

"Call from Nee-Yo-Been-So."

I have a half hour before school pickup. I look at my notebook. "Get work in FLA." I turn the TV on. *The Guiding Light.* I recognize these soap actors from when I was ten. *Family Feud.* Name something that breaks up couples. Cheating is the number-one answer. A commercial for lawyers. A commercial for airconditioning. A flurry of local ads geared for the elderly of Florida. The words *absorption, shingles, bunions, hemorrhoids, cysts, attorneys-at-law.* I turn it off. The phone rings. I try to get out of the room so the robot won't taunt me with her new mantra, "Call from Nee-Yo-Been-So."

It's my wife. I pick it up fast. "Hello, hello, hello."

I hear her voice but she can't hear me.

"Hello? Can you hear me?" I say with the panic of Dorothy in a twister.

She can't. She's there but she's not. I hang up and stay silent, awaiting the ring. The second the phone rings I pick it up. It's the kids' school. Alex is not in class.

"Not in class?" I ask.

"No, sir."

"Then where the hell is he?"

"I was hoping you knew."

"I dropped him there. I dropped him off at school this morning."

"I'm sure we'll find him," the woman says, and my mind plays with all the places he might be.

"There are woods behind the school, some kids go back there instead of class," she says.

"You think he's in the woods?"

"It's where kids cut class here."

"I'll call him and call you back," I say.

I call his number and get his voice mail. In the car my mind continues to play tricks. He's been kidnapped by a lunatic. He's fed up with this crappy idea to move to Florida and just walked off campus to join a cult. That meets in the woods. I walk into the school office and the woman tries to be comforting.

"Kids cut class," she says. "We'll find him."

I sit in the chair outside the principal's office and try his cell again. His voice mail picks up.

"Hi, it's Alex, leave a message."

"Hi, it's Dad, I'm looking for you. The school says you didn't show up. What's going on, big man? Call me as soon as you get this. Bye."

In the parking lot I call my wife, hoping she won't answer. I drive to the rear of the school and see the trees, the dense brush. No one is around. I get her voice mail and decide to drive home and see if he called the house line. Nausea rises in my stomach and chest and I swallow hard. I've fucking lost my son. I run into the house, avoiding my worst thoughts, and can't stop envisioning those parents on TV who plead for the return of their children. Is that me? Of course it's not me. No messages from Alex on the machine. I have to pick my daughter up from school so I'm back in the car. The sight of her gives me relief, but it turns to fear. I have only one kid. My phone rings; it's my wife.

"Hi," I say.

"The school called and said Alex wasn't in class," she says.

"I know, they called me too."

"Where is he, Jay?" she says.

"I'm looking for him, Jackie. I'm at the school and I'm looking for him."

"Do you have Tara?"

"Yes, yes I do. There's obviously no reason to panic."

"Did he just walk out of the school?"

"I don't know. I'll call you as soon as I find him."

And then I see him. Walking toward the car with his backpack over his shoulder. His face suggests nothing, a stoic, sleepy teenager. All my fears fall away, and I relish in the crumbling of the nightmare. My boy. His thin shoulders and thick brown hair. He opens the door, tosses the weighty backpack next to his sister, and plops down as if finally done with a long and rewarding day.

"How was school?" I ask.

"Good," he says, and puts his seat belt on without eye contact.

"Dad, can we stop at Yogurtology?" Tara asks.

"So it was good? It was fulfilling? You learned things?"

He glances at me. "Yes."

"Dad? Can we go to Yogurtology?"

"Sure, we can do that."

It's a chess game and I'm choosing to be patient. I drive a few blocks to the yogurt place and park. Alex doesn't want yogurt, says he'll sit in the car. I walk in with Tara and watch my son through the front window. His head is dipped, his eyes drained.

"Dad?" she says. "How many gummy bears can I get?"

I did this to him. Pulled him from the life he'd established, just to feel better about money, to assuage my own fears.

"I took ten, okay? I took ten gummy bears and now I'm gonna get ten M&M's, okay Dad?"

"Okay, baby. That sounds fine."

Through the window I see Alex open the car door. I'm baffled as to what he's doing.

"Hey!" I say, stepping outside. "Hey, Alex!"

"What?"

"Where are you going, man?"

He moves toward me. "Need to use the bathroom," he says and steps past me into the store.

The Woods Behind

| *Hot, muggy, like Africa in August*

I've decided the lizards outside my house are reincarnated felons of white crime. Something about their sallow cheeks and exposed wide eyes. Alone, I stare at two beneath the pool lounger, flaring their neck membranes between tiny push-ups. Chin to floor, their little elbows dipping. They freeze when they see me. I take out #79 and write the words *neck* and *membrane*. I check my phone. Alex's school hasn't called so I guess he's in class. My phone rings but it's my wife. She says she's coming home today, a day early. She'll be home in a few hours. She suggests we try to make a baby as soon as she walks in the door.

With my pants at my ankles and the sound of my belt clanging against the dishwasher I think of priorities and primitive needs. My wife is still wearing her jacket and I'm moving the toaster so we can use the kitchen counters. It's a Hollywood scene with moaning and dirty talk. We are not husband and wife but utter strangers in a kitchen. Nothing about our reality is invited to this fantastical whirlwind.

Until it ends.

We lie on the floor, silent, out of breath. The refrigerator changes gears and the ice machine drops a few.

"You didn't ask him where he went?" she says. "Not once?"

"I wanted to see if he'd tell me."

"He hardly speaks lately," she says.

"I know."

"Is our boy going to be okay?" she says.

I reach for my phone to see if the school called. "Of course he is."

She nods.

"How was your trip?"

"Productive," she says. "Smart people. Tired though. Have to be in Chicago on Monday, but only for two nights. Then I'm home for a while."

I guess I take a long deep breath. She faces me and her palm is on my chest. "You lonely?"

I shake my head.

"I was thinking," she says, "you should invite your New Jersey friends down here. Have them bring their wives and kids too. Have Michael and Joanna done the Orlando thing yet? Disney World? I know Tara would love to see the kids again. It might be good for Alex too. You can even invite Ray and Lizzie."

Ray's a guy I knew in high school. The type that peaks in his teens and falls terribly behind his friends as they age, mature, look for more lucrative and creative moments in life. We met in Little League, along with three other guys in our clique. I recall us, in 1985: the mullets, Ozzy and Ratt at the Meadowlands, my shitty used Honda. Ray dated a neighbor of mine, a girl named Jessica who was smart and funny and super sexy. I spent a lot of time envying him until Jessica and I made out in her dad's DeLorean. Ray was not happy. We braced to fight, fists formed, the whole thing. We ended up friends, not sure how. I think we shared sips of a bottle of Southern Comfort. After that, he was at my side like a loyal dog.

"I'll think about it," I say. "It would be three couples and their kids. Do we have room?"

My wife's phone rings. She finds it in her purse, four rings in. "It's the school," she says.

I sit up and stare at her.

"Hello?" she says, and listens.

She begins to shake her head. "Are you kidding me?" she says.

"What? I say. "What is it?"

"We'll be right there."

⚜   ⚜   ⚜

I pull behind the school and park next to the baseball field. Just beyond the centerfield fence is the football field. The woods run parallel to the bleachers and look as if they may be a mile deep. If you stand in front of the lane of trees you can see how dense the growth becomes. Jackie and I are out of the car, walking along the foul ground of the baseball field. Just over the left field wall we stand and look at the brush, the grassy path that leads inside.

"I'll go," I say. "You wait here."

"Why? I'll come with you," she says.

The trees hover over us and at times we're ducking, getting wet from the dew on the branches. A full hundred yards in I see a person with brown hair. He's sitting on a log in front of an unlit campfire, his phone held inches from his nose. It's my son. I turn around, tap my wife on the shoulder, and point at him. She makes a noise from her mouth.

"Let me go talk to him," I say.

"Okay. Don't scare him." She looks his way and nods.

I walk closer, trying not to startle him. I make it almost there until the crunch of my steps give me away.

He stands, his jaw open, then gathers his backpack.

"I was heading to class," he says.

I sit on the log and pat the spot next to me. "Sit."

"I have to get back," he says.

"Just sit, okay?"

He removes the backpack and lowers himself again.

"Tell me what you're doing out here," I say.

He says nothing, looks drained, defeated.

"Why are you out here during school?"

He dips his head and seems to swallow before his shoulders jerk forward and he cries, a flooding of pain. I hold him and he allows me to, a rare softening in the tension of his body.

"They tease me," he says.

"Who teases you?"

"All of them. I hate this school. The teachers, the kids, I *hate* it."

"I didn't know."

"That jackass from New York I told you about. He makes fun of me and all his friends laugh. I tried to make it better but it made it worse."

"What did you do to make it better?"

"I talked to him."

"Good for you."

"It made it worse."

"In what way?"

He shakes his head. "Forget it. I'm stuck," he says. "They think I'm a loser."

"You're anything but a loser."

He cries again.

I hold him close to me. His mother joins us on the log. He stands when he sees her, tries to get his bearings, lifts his book bag. She hugs him but he's embarrassed, fidgety. "Forget it," he says and starts to walk away, his eyes streaming.

"How about you take the day off?" my wife says.

He stops, nods, is relieved. We all walk out of the woods. A class of kids is on the baseball field as we pass. I see all of them as the culprit, the jerks who called my son a loser and laughed at him. His head stays low as we pass them. I fantasize that suddenly a pretty girl will yell, "Hi Alex, see you at lunch," but it doesn't happen. Jackie takes him to the car and I go in the school to say we found him. And that we're heading home today.

In the car we're silent. I find him in the rearview and see tears in his eyes. His skin is pale, his expression so flat, drained.

"How are we going to handle this?" Jackie says.

"You can't help me."

"That's not true," she says.

"I don't want to talk about it."

"Alex?" she says, turning her body to face him.

He rubs his eyes with the heels of both palms. I stop the car at a red light and his mother looks at him again. "The more you can share about what's going on and how you're feeling . . . the better."

I see him looking out the window, blinking, trying to find words. "At night, in bed," he says, just above a whisper, "I think about losing you. Dying. Sometimes funerals."

Jackie and I look at each other.

"Funerals, buddy?" I ask.

"I think about Mom on airplanes and crashing and stuff."

"But they're so safe," Jackie says.

"I know. I can't help it."

I drive all the way to the house. My lips are dry, my heart like a brick. Alex is the first to get out of the car. We watch him use his own key to get inside. I look at Jackie, her face so pinched.

"I'll call my mother," I say.

Mother Immunity

My mother went back to school in the late seventies and got a PhD in psychology. When depression walloped me in college she bought me a natural herb called St. John's wort. It got me clearer and I took it for years after when I felt low for whatever reason. I used to believe my depression was from growing up without a father. My mom explained I probably had the depression gene. Perhaps my beautiful son has it too. As I brace to tell her the truth about Alex, I worry the words I choose will only scare her. I remember how worried she was when I left home for college, sending me weekly articles on colon and testicular cancer. No matter what mood I might be in, there they awaited in my mailbox, death prevention. She also sent me articles about rubbers and STDs. When the SARS scare ran into Y2K I just stopped opening the envelopes. I hear you, my sweet mother. You fear things that can wipe me out. I am one of your offspring. You will wither away if the disease that ultimately kills me was on your radar and you never emailed about it.

My mother is not the little gray lady one imagines. No afghan yet, no drooling, no dentures. The reason she's still attractive in her seventies is probably due to all the articles on herbs and mushrooms she's taken to heart. Everytime we speak she wants me to know that her father died five days before my birth from colon cancer and it's about time I allowed someone to cram a scope up my asshole. It's hard to explain how the heterosexual male feels about his asshole. If you put too much effort into describing it, you sound like a homophobe or a Republican.

I dial her number and she picks up right away. "I was just going to call you," she says. "Listen to me, it's going to be a bit uncomfortable but it's absolutely crucial that you go get a colonoscopy because your grandfather died five days before your birth; I had just buried him. Please tell me you won't ignore it."

"I told you I would see a doctor."

"Tell your doctor in California to send your records to Florida."

"I can handle it, Mother."

"Good, thank you, don't wait too long."

"Mom?"

"Yes, love?"

"I think Alex is showing signs of depression."

Silence. Then, "Damn it. He needs to be on St. John's wort. If that doesn't give him relief he'll need to see a psychiatrist for a prescription and take that simultaneously while seeing a therapist. I can recommend a good person. It could be his diet, new pressures, the transition to Florida."

"I think it's the move."

"Do you eat quinoa?"

"Do I eat what?"

"Quinoa!" she says, pronouncing it *keenwa*.

I envision a large jar of whatever it is in my mailbox on Thursday. I see it filled with multicolored corn that's been marinated in the placenta-sac of a cow. After drying, remove each kernel and place it under your tongue while sitting under a banyan tree. You will live longer than Yoda.

"It's for his well-being and immunity. Can I send you some?"

The last weird-sounding herb she sent me was for nausea, shingles, and dysentery, I think. I sprinkled it on my cereal while my wife laughed. I ate all of it and actually got a little light-headed before falling asleep in the living room for four hours.

"Google it," my mother says.

"I will."

"Just Google it."

Quinoa originated in the Andean region of Ecuador, Bolivia, Colombia, and Peru, where it was successfully domesticated three to four thousand years ago for human consumption. I skim soil requirements, agronomy, harvesting, and handling. Handling involves threshing the seed heads and winnowing the seed to remove the husk. Before storage, the seeds need to be dried in order to avoid germination.

I find St. John's wort and quinoa in Whole Foods. Alex won't take either so I decide to sneak the quinoa onto his cereal. If it helps his brain, his mood, the depression, then my behavior can't be considered underhanded. I eat it, Jackie eats it, and I get my daughter to try some too. Her tongue comes out like a turtle's head. The tip bumps the quinoa. She likes it. She takes a bite. I am positive I just added fifteen to twenty years to her life and enough serotonin to get her through her forties. I feel badly about sneaking it on Alex. I offer him money to try it.

"I don't want it."

"It's for your happiness."

"It looks gross."

"It's meant to help you feel more clear and alive."

"It looks weird."

"Just try a little," my wife says. "If you don't like it, don't eat it."

He does. Not so bad. He likes it.

I call my mother back to tell her Alex tried it. Turns out she just finished an article that says quinoa, taken in high amounts, can cause irritable bowel syndrome in less than 3 percent of users. There is a pause between us, as I pick the seeds from my teeth.

"But honey," she says, "have you heard of this mushroom called *Agaricus blazei* Murrill? I think Alex might like it."

"No, Mother."

"Google it."

Also known as *Agaricus brasiliensis*, the mushroom is a front-runner in cancer research. Immortality in a mushroom.

I buy two and a half pounds of the stuff but Alex refuses to try it. I buy a grinder and turn some to powder to make it less ugly. I pay him and he smells it. Ten more bucks and it's in his mouth. I call my mother to tell her we all tried it, even Alex. I can hear her smiling through the phone. At least her youngest son and his family will never, ever die.

The Clique

| *Rainy, sunny, rainy, overcast, sunny, and now some lightning*

Here's who comes to visit us in Florida. Michael Highland, his wife Joanna, their two kids Farley and Harper; my friend Nicholas Bryant and his wife Gigi and their two kids Adam and Sasha; Ray, his girlfriend Lizzie, and their daughter Katrina. They all pour out of a maroon rental bus. Lizzie looks pissed off already. In high school I had science with her and remember how she slept and snored in class. Right around the time Jackie got pregnant with Tara I received a call from Ray. Lizzie Thompson was pregnant with his baby. At the time he was unemployed, drinking a ton, and had stopped calling any of us, his friends. Lizzie approaches me and I say hi and kiss her cheek.

"Nice to see you again, Lizzie," I say. She's clutching her bed pillow with both arms.

"Can I use your bathroom?" she asks and takes her daughter by the hand.

"Of course. Just inside. Hi, Katrina. Remember me?" I say.

"My daddy says you write commercials for the radio."

"I did. I did do that for a while. Not anymore. Are you a writer?"

She nods and her mother snorts. "She never stops."

"I stop, Mom."

"Let's use the bathroom," Lizzie says.

Ray gives me a bear hug and lifts me off the ground. My arms are being pinched in the loving exchange. When he returns me to earth I have to rub them. We all met in Little League and played for the Chamber of Commerce. Nicholas Bryant, a lawyer now, was on our team too. When we were ten, he asked me if I wanted to see his dad's porno movies. It turned out I really did. I invited the third baseman, Ray, and our catcher, Michael, who is now a pediatrician in Manhattan. I was the shortstop. Ray was our best hitter and in high school was the best at getting girls. His car was perfect, his clothes, the way he chewed gum, it all helped his love life. I could see he was on top of the world, but he was actually peaking. Problem was he was seventeen and not going anywhere after graduation. The rest of us went to college, formed relationships, took jobs, and bought homes. Ray was always in town, waiting for his friends to return so we could get smashed during Thanksgiving week. As we got older we stopped seeing him when we returned for holidays. Rumors arose: he was in Detroit working for Ford, he was in Atlanta building houses. When he got Lizzie pregnant he stopped leaving and found a job as a mechanic in town. When I offered to fly the three of them to Florida for the reunion, he was overjoyed, honored, told me I was always his best friend. Michael approaches me with his arms in the air, an all-encompassing smile.

"Hello," I announce. "Welcome to sunny Florida."

"There he is, there he is," Michael says.

Michael, Ray, and Nicholas come at me for a group hug. Our arms are linked like rugby players'.

"Hi guys," I say, and feel a comfort I wasn't expecting.

"Don't let go yet," Michael says.

"Get your pinkie out of my butt, Ray," Nick says.

"I thought it was your vagina," says Ray.

It's long now, the hug. I'm getting hot. But the contact is important, the friendship, the memories of ourselves so young. I know I'll have these people in my life when I'm ninety. Tara comes out and greets everyone. It's so sweet to see my daughter kissing and hugging my friends' small kids.

"We have a pool," she says to the gaggle.

"Get your bathing suits on!" shouts Nick.

The large group moves inside. My wife begins to embrace everyone in the kitchen. She was closest with Joanna and Gigi in the days we still lived in New Jersey. Joanna was her maid of honor. She and Lizzie despise one another, so it's awkward, for a second. It began when Jackie saw Lizzie smoking a cigarette during her pregnancy with Katrina. My wife slapped it out of her mouth and Lizzie went after her and shoved her into me. It's stupid now, time to move on. I watch Lizzie ignore Jackie during all this hugging and greeting. Oh well. Jackie, Gigi, and Joanna find me alone in the living room.

"What's wrong with Lizzie?" Gigi asks.

"I have no idea. Probably a fight with Ray. It's what they do."

"Should I offer her a beer?" my wife says. "She's just standing in the kitchen."

I'm pleased she's being so thoughtful. Liz might be her least favorite person. It's not Jackie's fault, she just can't stomach shitty parenting. Katrina runs into the room wide-eyed. She's chasing my daughter but stops to hug me. "I'm so glad you're here," I yell as she runs away, toward the kitchen. "We're gonna have so much fun!"

"Stop running!" barks Lizzie from the kitchen. "Follow me."

In come Lizzie and a deflated Katrina. Lizzie's long sandy hair is in a ball on her head. Her sweatpants are pink and say *Juicy* on the tush. Her Crocs are orange. "Any of you seen Ray?"

Katrina is suddenly younger than her age. She lowers her eyes, uncertain how to react.

"He's outside," I say. "With Michael by the pool. How have you been, Liz?"

She shrugs, almost taken aback by the "interview." No one ever asks her how she's doing, what she's doing.

"Good," she says, and glances warily at Gigi.

Silence.

"Katrina," my daughter yells. "This way!"

"Can I go, Mom?" she asks Lizzie.

Lizzie grabs Katrina's backpack strap. "Why you still got this thing on, Katrina? Are you a zombie? Take it off already." Katrina removes the backpack. Lizzie shakes her head, incredulous. My wife announces a tour and Joanna and Gigi walk up the stairs. Perhaps they're running from Lizzie, I don't know, don't care. Kids are everywhere and my daughter is thrilled, running from room to room with her ponytail hopping. My son assesses all the bodies and I can see it's overwhelming for him. He asks Farley and Harper if they want to see his room. I'm proud of him for trying, for rising above.

Everyone wants to swim. I head outdoors with Michael and Ray. We sit on lawn chairs and watch everyone jump in. The splashes and young voices help ease the sudden silence between us. Ray and Michael were best friends in the eighties. All the old photographs have the two of them arm in arm. Michael went to college, became a doctor, met his wife in school, and landed in New York. Ray didn't.

"I've missed you guys," I say.

Ray rests his hand on his belly while watching the kids. "Dare me to cannonball on top of all of 'em?"

"I really miss you too," Michael says. "You been well? You copywriting?"

I nod, recognizing how foreign it is to be asked about my work. I think about showing him #79 and the short personal essay I wrote last week. "Been thinking about maybe publishing something funny. Creative and funny."

"Great, can I hear it?" asks Michael.

Ray removes his T-shirt and tosses it over his shoulder. In his jeans he darts for the pool and jumps, tucks, and explodes into the water with a *kaboom* that leaves the water tossing and the kids diving for cover. Michael has wet shoes, my daughter is laughing, and Katrina, the only victim, is gripping her left knee and crying.

"What?" says Ray. "Don't tell me I got ya. Oh, I got ya, Kat?"

Katrina limps out of the pool. "Mommy!" But Lizzie's inside. I walk to her and put a towel around her. "Ow, ow, it hurts," she says and Ray approaches.

"I didn't see you," he says, like a child.

"Doesn't matter if you saw her or not," Michael says. "You landed on her."

"I didn't try to."

"But you did."

"It feels better now," Katrina says, uninterested in listening to her father fight with his friend. She gets up and starts to limp inside.

"You okay, Katrina?" my daughter says.

Katrina nods. Ray follows her in, dripping all the way.

Michael sits up from his lounger and places his feet on the ground. His arms fold, his lips straighten. "What a colossal idiot," he says. "Anyway, you were telling me about your writing."

"I'm just messing around with my notebook. Sometimes the pieces are pretty good."

"Read me one."

Wasn't expecting to be sharing it but I'm light on my feet as I run to grab #79. It's different when you share something like this with a friend who actually reads and loves books. When I get back Michael is helping Harper with her goggles. She runs off when he's done and flops in the pool.

"Go ahead," he says, "I'm listening."

As I read the piece I notice Michael's reactions. Nodding, even gripping the tip of his goatee. But as I continue I begin to worry that the story is slow, even trite and derivative, wobbly in its limited scope. I'm listening to myself talking and now wondering if my voice is growing quiet as I forge on through the muck of my stringy, drawn-out thoughts.

"I love it!" he says, and Nick's kids and Tara all land in the pool at once. The splash reaches our feet again.

"Hey," he says. "Look out for my toes, you animals."

The fact that he can just roll on with his life, without a word about the essay. Did he hear me? He's the only friend I have who's ever written anything. He was an English major at Colgate. I think my writing sucks. Why did I bring it up? Why didn't I just keep it to myself where it would remain a mere notion of endless possibility? Instead I just read pure, dimensionless bullshit. To a person who isn't fooled.

My daughter, dripping wet, hands Michael a pool toy to throw.

"In the shallow end," she says. "I can't go that deep yet."

He tosses the rings. "How's that?"

"Good," Tara says, and pinches her nose before jumping in.

My wife and Joanna stroll the yard, pointing at the tops of palm trees. Michael is oblivious, finished with my idea. Nothing I said to him is germinating; not a thing I uttered has resonated in his mind. I look at him, smiling as he does, so much fun. He needs to stop throwing the rings now. He needs to let himself come back to that moment when I knew I had him, listening. Why? Because he loves me, knows me, cares for me, has put me on that list of people he'll go out of his way for. He just has to let what I've read sink in. It might not be that bad. Is the idea good or not? He won't stop playing with my daughter, his friends, his kids. He's acting as if he arrived in Florida for nothing more than some relaxation. Now he stands and makes his way to the side of the pool.

"I like it," he finally says. "But I thought you said it was funny."

"Come in the pool, Daddy!" my daughter says.

"What are you waiting for, Jay?" says Nick.

"Maybe he doesn't want to get his hair wet," says Ray and all the kids laugh.

This latest essay is over, killed, dumped, fucked, and burned. And the panic and pain inside me are doused for a second by the notion of a clean slate. I'll start something new. I close #79 and see my son inside the house, sitting alone, his phone lighting his face. I walk in, grab his hand, and start to pull him outside. He locks his feet, yanks his hand away. "Get the *hell* off me!" he screams as loud as he can. Everyone hears this, looks inside at us. I let go of him, shocked he'd bark like that.

Lizzie is there with Katrina behind her. She nods with satisfaction, eating a plum.

"You heard him," Lizzie says, swiping the juice from her chin with a smirk. "Get the hell off."

Her teeth are beige, her scrunchy red. Alex walks past her and to his room. Lizzie uses her thumb like a hitchhiker, pointing at his back. "Aren't they so cute at this age?" she says, bonding with me.

I nod and Katrina says, "Can I see your notebook?"

I hand it to her. She rests her open hand on top and looks up at me with a smile.

"Will you read me something?"

The Tree

I n the morning, the plan is to visit the Mahanley River. The guidebook says it's one of two non-ocean swimming spots that are free of alligators and it's only a twenty-minute drive. Michael says he was there when he was fourteen or so and he remembers a banyan tree with branches that hang out over the water. He tells Alex and Nick's son Adam that they can get "serious air," if they're brave enough to leap and let go at the right time. I drive my car with Michael and Joanna and their kids and Nick takes the rental bus with his wife and kids as well as Ray, Lizzie, and Katrina. When we arrive there's a marked path that leads to a beach of sorts with rocky cliffs to the right and left. The walk is longer than Tara and Katrina realized and they both have beach chairs on their backs.

"Keep it up, we're close," Michael says and we all moan at him in various ways.

Ray announces he's going to run ahead to see just how far it is. He offers to carry half the chairs and both Tara and Katrina take advantage. Sweating like mad, Ray flexes all his aging muscles and groans as he stands from a squat.

"I'll be back," he says and starts to jog ahead, looking like a hunchback Sherpa.

Jackie, Gigi, and Joanna are carrying two coolers and all the towels. I take a couple off the top to relieve the load.

"I don't remember this long walk at all," Michael says.

"We know," his wife says. "We know you don't remember. I bet it wasn't this hot either. You were probably here in the winter. Visiting your grandmother."

"Yes, it was winter break."

Everyone moans.

I see the sand, it's all good. The walk was a bit long but flat, no complaints. Tough to make everyone happy when fifteen people have opinions. Ray is near the water, kneeling and talking to someone. He's still wearing all the chairs. When I get closer I see it's Tara's friend Ginger and her mother, the pretty blond lady from the no zone at school. When she sees me she lights up, her mouth open, her glasses removed. I smile back but I'm forgetting her name and need to introduce her to my wife, of course. They shake hands and I do that oblivious pause we all do, as if I've forgotten the protocol for introductions. Ginger's mom finally says, "I'm Teri."

"I'm Jackie," my wife says.

Tara is so happy to see Ginger and Ginger and Katrina are wearing the same bathing suit with a cartoon whale on the front. Teri asks if we're going to the Daddy-Daughter Dance and I end up buying tickets from her on the beach. I learn Teri runs all social events for the school, K through six. She tells us that Teri's brother will be taking Ginger to the dance, as she is divorced and her husband estranged.

The water is light blue, my great friends are here and relaxed, and there's a slight and intermittent breeze on my forehead, reminding me that some days are abundant with perfection. Jackie introduces our friends to Ginger's mom—I mean Teri. A circle of beach chairs forms and I reach for a Coke from the cooler but grab two. Where is my Coca-Cola-loving thirteen-year-old man? I look around and finally see him up on the cliffs to our right. He sits perched, his arms wrapped around his knees, and he's staring out at the river, the sky beyond. Hovering over him is the enormous banyan tree Michael remembered. I remove my phone to see if I'm close enough for a photo. I'm not. These trees are famous for their chunky exposed roots that coil up from the ground like earthy electrical wires. My boy looks small amid the drama.

Ray and Lizzie sit a good ten feet away from everyone else. They're both sipping from a thermos that Lizzie's been clutching since we left the house. Nicky's kids are in the water and now Tara and Katrina are in too. Jackie and I throw a blanket down on the sand next to Michael and Joanna, who are next to Nick and Gigi. Everyone sees a flying fish and the girls run screaming from the water. I have to laugh; the fish was the size of a Wheat Thin. Ray pretends to attack the fish and tells the girls to watch him catch it. They all stare at the wild man thrashing around in the water. Once again, the lunatic draws attention to the child within him. He stands from the water, pretends to track the fish, and then belly flops in very shallow water. The kids are roaring. Farley, Harper, Adam, Sasha, and Tara cannot catch their breath. When he sees the reaction he just keeps going. I can see his chest is red, looks slapped and raw. Lizzie is shaking her head, sipping off the thermos. My wife mumbles, "Moron," and the other wives laugh.

"Okay, man," I yell. "Looks like that fish is too fast for you."

"What do you mean, jellybean?" he says and exhibits the most violent of his cartoonish body flops. I can only wince. I look up at my son to see if he's watching this ridiculous yet funny display of Ray's personality. He hasn't moved. I stand with my Coke and walk to the back of the beach, near his perch on the cliffs. I raise the can to see if I can bait him to join us.

"Alex! Want one of these?"

He either doesn't hear me or chooses not to.

Ray dries off as the kids stop laughing. Nick's boy Adam has never seen anything that funny in his life. His mother, Gigi, is giving him juice to settle his stomach.

"Alex!" I yell.

"What's he doing up there?" Ray asks, dabbing his armpits.

"Being alone," I say. "He's okay."

Ray squints up at Alex and tosses his towel over my shoulder. He then climbs, without shoes, up the side of the cliff and plops his ass down next to Alex. I can't hear them. I decide a conversation with Ray could be good for him. Or not. I walk back to the group, and Joanna is pissed off at Michael for staring at Ginger's mom's body as she went in for a swim.

"I wasn't even looking at her, Joanna!"

"You were staring at her ass the entire time. Until I called you on it you were gawking at her. It's embarrassing."

"For who?" Nick says. "It's a beach. There aren't rules about who you can and can't look at."

"But he's gawking," Joanna says.

"Gawking? I was *not* gawking."

Teri dips herself in the water and walks back. None of us want to get caught looking at her. Her body is one of those "great job,

God" forms that's worth taking a glance at if you have a heartbeat. The bikini is pure white and the tan is Florida's own. I'm digging through the cooler so I cannot be accused.

"How old do you think she is?" Nicky says.

"Early forties."

"Enough, guys," Joanna says. "Anyone want lunch?"

Katrina and Tara approach the "adult area" and I see Katrina is holding a hot pink notebook and looking at me. I ask her about it and she's sitting next to me, so sweet, and removes an enormous pencil from her bag. We laugh at the size of it and she says the eraser is removable. She asks if I brought #79 and I didn't. I'm told I can share her book and am handed an equally large pencil.

"I have this great game," she says. "Want to play?"

"Okay," I say.

"I'll write the first sentence and then you come in and write the second, and so on, okay? Tara, you can play too. But I only have two pencils. I'll write the first sentence," she says and dips her head and torso over the notebook and begins to write.

I look back and up at Alex and Ray. Ray is tugging on the branch of the banyan tree. Alex stands with him.

"Okay, read this and add to it," Katrina says.

There once was a prince named August who had two dogs, a cow named Moo-moo, eleven chickens, and a scooter with two broken wheels.

I read about August and decide the prince needs a friend.

Prince August was a lonely soul so he married a woman the locals called Crazy Annie. She thought

Moo-moo might be yummy for dinner but that didn't
fix his scooter.

"Your turn," I say.

"Already? Wow, fast."

Now I'm worried I hurried it.

"What did you write, Dad?" Tara says.

"You have to read it."

I hand Katrina the pad and she pushes her sunglasses up on
her forehead. She lowers her eyes to read my part. A smile forms
before freezing on her face. I guess I did okay. Katrina writes for
about five minutes, giggling all the while. At one point she removes
the sunglasses from her head and has them in her mouth.

"Show us, Katrina," Tara says.

"Okay."

Crazy Annie and Prince August arrived at the scooter
store. They sat for a while and August told her the
truth. "I have ten other wives," he admitted. "I also have
two dogs and eleven chickens." Crazy Annie laughed
and said, "Wow, you must have a really big bed."

I laugh when I read this. With my head back I laugh and close
my eyes. It feels great. The sun on my face is shaded by someone.
I look up. It's Alex.

"Hey, man, want a Coke?"

"Can I talk to you?"

"Of course."

My wife stands and approaches and she's got her hand on his
back, moving him away from the group.

"I want to go home," he says, trying to hold back tears.

I look up at the banyan tree and Ray is preparing to launch himself off the cliff and into the water.

"What happened?"

My son looks up at Ray and the tears rise. "He said I was a pussy if I didn't swing off that branch."

"He called you a pussy?" my wife says.

He nods.

Jackie is on her way up the cliff.

"I'll talk to him, honey," I say. "Jackie, let me talk to him."

She doesn't listen. I know her. She's going to blame Ray for all the bullying Alex is seeing at school. In her head she's about to fix Alex by scolding my stupid high school friend.

Alex takes a deep breath. "I just don't feel like doing it right now. I'd do it. I will do it. I just felt pressured and I kept saying no and he was like, 'Let's do it together, everyone will cheer for us, you'll prove you have balls.' And I said no, I don't feel like it right now."

"Just forget it," I say. "Looks dangerous to me."

"I will next time," he says, scratching his right forearm.

"Or not."

"I will, Dad. I will do it. I'm not scared."

Jackie reaches the top of the cliff just in time for Ray to swing out over the beach and let go. He attempts a flip but doesn't have time and lands on his head in the water. Lizzie stands when she sees this, probably not sure if the father of her child survived the fall. But of course Ray stands, rubbing his lower back. Jackie is on her way down the cliff and into the water. She confronts him, his smile and accomplishment fading. He stands a foot taller than my wife but with her hands on her hips and her chin tilted just so, she is treating him to a barrage of discouraging words.

Michael approaches us. "What's Jackie saying to him?" he says.

"I don't know," I say.

Alex closes his eyes, humiliated. Ray steps around my wife in the water, a scolded dog.

"Alex?" I say.

He faces me.

"Want to swim with me?"

"No."

"Let's take a walk," I say.

"No."

Ray walks to us. "Your mom says I hurt your feelings."

"No, not really," says Alex. "I just don't feel like it today."

"Fine, no problem, I just thought we'd do it together and shock everyone."

"I'm tired today," Alex says.

Ray ruffles Alex's hair. "You be your own man. Don't let anyone pressure you into anything."

Alex forces a smile.

"Now your dad here better follow me up there because it's time for him to fly like a birdie."

I shake my head. "Not happening, go bug your other friends. No flying for me."

Ray throws his hand at me and walks to ask Michael and Nick. He finds no takers. So he heads up there again, gets a solid grip on the branch, and this time lands on his back. We all think he might be dead. But he rises from the water with both hands on his butt.

Lizzie slowly stands from her towel and walks toward us. She has a cigarette in her mouth and the thermos in her clutch.

"Where do you pee around here?" she says.

I point at the water. She looks at me like I just suggested she poop in the street. But then she shuffles to the water's edge and passes Ray without a word. She flicks the cigarette and squats like a catcher. What a princess.

"Can we go home soon, Dad?" Alex says.

All the wives see Lizzie and now they're looking back at me. I shrug as Ray climbs the cliff again.

"Your turn, Jay," Katrina says, waving her enormous pencil. "I think you're going to like what I wrote."

Night-Light

The fish tank in my daughter's room was a gift from my father-in-law. It is beautiful to me: the idea of water as canvas, active and varying, always in color. It's a tropical tank so the fish are small and bright, sometimes neon. The ritual at bedtime is for me to read to her a bit before I feed them. I then turn her lights out but keep the bulb in the tank on. I cherish the moments we're both on her bed, allowing our eyes to track the sinking food, the darting fish. Tonight Katrina is on the trundle bed. She's reading her notebook to herself, the adventures of Moo-moo and the prince.

"Look at Meatball," Tara says. "He's always hogging the food."

Katrina looks up. "He's hungry tonight."

"He's always hungry. He eats all of it."

She's right. I think about adding a bit more but see Spaghetti Face, face up. He's quite dead among the plastic orange leaves, hidden, thankfully, near the surface. In my experience as a father I've learned that death on any level is a terrible subject for bedtime. I add a dab of food and we watch Meatball race for it like Jaws after Richard Dreyfuss.

"Selfish," my daughter says and settles into her bed, truly tired after a full day of visiting and swimming. She tugs her sheet higher, up near her chin. On her side she yawns and shuts her eyes for a second, treasuring the comfort. I stare at her, my girl, her pure blond hair, her little shoulders, the faded purple nightgown. It's love in ways untold. The power of it is rooted in the heart, I think, because that's where I would die if she ever ceased to exist. There is no before her. There is only now and the rest of her days, which must outlast mine. The bubbling from the fish tank filter is loud when you focus on it. She is used to the white noise. I kiss her near her left eye, my nose touching her eyebrow.

"I love you."

"You're stubbly," she whispers.

I touch my face. "Sorry."

"It's okay," she says. "Hall light and ladybug."

I kneel and kiss Katrina on her head.

"Can we write one more time before bed?" she says.

"Tomorrow. Tomorrow we can write about Moo-moo."

"Aww."

I walk out and flip the hall light on. I keep the door half open and there's a pink ladybug night-light.

"Good night," I say.

"Good night, Daddy," she mumbles.

"Good night, Daddy," Katrina says and the girls giggle.

On my way upstairs I poke my head in on Alex. He's awake, sitting with his head on his desktop.

"You okay?"

"Tired."

I sit on his bed. "Can I tuck you in?" I ask, and wish I'd used other words.

"No."

"Sorry."

"Dad?"

"Yes?"

"Where do you think we go when we die?"

I reach for his knee and he moves it. "I don't know, exactly, buddy. I think it might end there. What are your thoughts?"

"I think, I'm glad I'm not your age."

"Uh-huh. Closer to old age, I see. But you know, I still have lots of time."

He snorts out of his nose and looks at me. "That's just it. You don't have a lot of time at all. I have so much more than you."

I nod.

"So," he says, swallowing his fear. "Aren't you scared?"

"I guess . . . I try to live for now."

He sniffs, taking this in. "I'm going to miss you when you pass away," he says, not facing me.

I smile, sort of, and take his hand in mine. "Thank you. But I have more time than you think. And I always eat all my asparagus."

"Daddy," says Tara. She and Katrina are standing in their nightgowns, both giggling, with notebooks and pencils.

"I said tomorrow. Now go back to bed, you crazy girls."

"Just one round," Katrina says.

I kiss my son on his cheek. "I'll be right back." He doesn't respond.

I walk the girls back and bump into Ray and Michael. They want to go out and drink somewhere. I try to talk them out of it but now Nicky is into the idea too.

I say yes to a round of Katrina's game. By the time the guys are dressed to go out, Moo-moo and the prince own a Hummer outlet in Reno and are selling gas guzzlers to Taylor Swift and Iggy Azalea. The moms finally get the girls back to bed, and I return to Alex's room. He's on his bed, eyes closed. I look at my son, his beautiful face. I kiss his forehead to warm his fears, to fight off the shadows.

In the front hallway Ray smells like too much Old Spice. He has his arm around me and now I smell like musk too.

"I hear St. Petersburg has one hell of a nightlife," he says. "You ready to prove it?"

I look at my watch, and then my friends.

"Why not."

Night Cap

FRIDAY NIGHT | *Light rain*

We end up in a bar called Willy's Sports, about two miles from my house. Somehow Lizzie stayed home after a quick but upsetting shouting match that ended with her threatening to take Katrina to a motel. Katrina heard none of it but we all got to see what her life must be like at home. Ray is still pissed off in the car, rumbling about the lack of time he has to himself. Nicky has a joint and we smoke it, passing it around. I envision the Floridian cop who arrests us, six foot six, a shaved head and a black gun. I see Ray killing him and the car screeching away. The weed is making me paranoid. About cops. My son. My work. My worth.

"Hey, Nicky," I say.

"Yes?"

"It's weed, right, nothing else?"

"Of course, man! Ya think I'd dose you? It's called Sour Diesel. Has a kick, right?"

Michael agrees. "I'm pretty fucked up."

Ray laughs and rolls the window down. "You guys are such puss —" he says, stopping himself and looking at me with apologetic eyes. "Sorry, man. Again, sorry that came out with Alex. I was being casual, ya know? Don't be such a puss."

"Okay, okay," I say. "I just want to get out and park this car. Do you think we smell?"

"Yes," says Nicky. "We smell like Sour Diesel."

I'm too high. The parking attendant is a ghoul with green skin. We walk through an alley and out to the street where the masses comfort me. So many women dressed to the nines in heels and Chihuly-inspired dresses. Ray is psyched for all the eye candy and I'm proud of St. Petersburg for its nightlife and sexual energy. Even if none of us can touch any of it. Strangely, Ray *is* touching a woman, just outside the bar. He leans in to tell her something and she laughs. The four of us can't believe it. Ray's still got it. Our sheepish, stoned glances at each other make me feel pathetic and I know I've never been this baked in my life.

We walk into the bar and I can hear the air-conditioning humming in my eardrum. Why is my hearing heightened? This better just be weed I smoked. Ray is leaning over the bar, talking closely to the attractive bartender, shaping his mouth like Andrew McCarthy's in *Pretty in Pink*. I guess he's on the prowl. I guess when one impregnates Lizzie Thompson there's still room for dating others. Forget the fact that he's wearing a green Jets sweatshirt with a hood and hasn't shaved since his arrival. Once a warrior of the suburban summer, he used to have abs that could be seen from the funnel cake cart in Belmar.

"Hey," Ray calls to the bartender.

She faces him.

"Anyone ever tell you you look like Angelina Jolie?"

The woman snorts and looks at me. "All the time," she says sarcastically. She does not resemble the actress.

Nick puts his hand on Ray's shoulder and guides him away from whatever bullshit he's spewing.

"What are you doing?" Ray says.

"I want to sit," Nick says. "Let's go find a booth."

"The bar, bro, the bar is fine," Ray says. "I like that chick. I was talking to her."

"She's working and your fiancée is eight blocks from here. Be normal." Michael helps Nick push Ray away from the bar.

Ray takes a hard swing at Michael's grip on his sweatshirt. "Get the fuck off."

He gives him the finger and heads back to the bar. I stand there and stew in the moment. I smell wet rug, Axe deodorant, and spicy chicken wings. The bartender is busy now, so Ray waits, lifts his drink to her, leans there like an aging John Wayne. I tell him I'm going to join the boys and sit near the front. Ray waits and waits for her. The bartender is ignoring him. I get his attention and wave him over. He finally strolls over, sits with a thump, and throws his drink back.

"You look like someone just hacked your nuts off," he says to Nick.

"You can do what you want, Ray," Nick says. "I'm not your dad."

"Thank God. Just stay out of my grill. You were always like that. Meddling. Pulling me away. I'm a man, ya know? We aren't teenagers. Right?"

"Let's say she falls in love with you," Nick says. "Something you say makes her drop everything. She hops over the bar, tells her boss to stick it, and she's ready. Where are you fornicating with this person? At Jay's house? In front of all our families? Maybe you don't consider your family important enough."

Ray stands and stares down at Nick. "What did you say?"

"Okay, okay, shut the hell up," I offer.

"What the hell is it Nick's business if I want to get laid?" Ray says. "And no, I wouldn't take her to Jay's house. Think I'm an asshole? Do you?"

"Listen, it's your life, man," Nick says.

"I'd go back to her house."

"Well then, get out there, ya know? Ask someone to dance," says Michael. "We'll watch."

"I like the bartender."

"She's working," says Nick. "Choose someone else."

"These girls aren't as hot as the chicks outside," he says. "Where are all the hot girls, man? This bar sucks."

I look at my watch. "It's early."

"Yeah, well, I don't need this shit," he says. "I fly all the way down here and I don't see one hot babe. In Florida."

Teetering on only the rear two legs of his chair, he tips the last of his drink back and surveys the prospects.

"Ugly, fat, taken, taken, ugly. *Auuughh!*"

Ray falls back off his chair. He tries to catch himself but can't and crashes on the floor.

"You okay?" I say.

People look, laugh quietly.

He just lies there with ice cubes on his chest. He says nothing. Michael and Nick can't help but laugh. They point, laugh more, and high five. Ray was always the guy who wouldn't shut up until he got humbled, in front of everyone. Nick leans in to whisper in my ear. He tells me he stuck his toe under Ray's chair and dumped him with a flick of his foot. I help Ray stand and pat him with napkins. We both begin to laugh. I worshipped this man in high school. He was the big brother I'd never get from my big brother. He knew so much, drove so fast. I had no idea he was in the midst of realizing all he'd ever achieve. It must be such a letdown for Ray, after so much promise, so much horsepower in his Camaro. Now he's an unemployed father, with Lizzie at his side.

The tequila shots arrive. He wants to toast. Mostly, he just wants to ensure we all drink ours too. Alas, he's sentimental.

"There will never be a better night in our lives," he says, and his old smile appears, the faded dimples trying to wink from his cheeks. With his endorphins firing he throws the first one back and makes the classic cringing face. We all reluctantly do our shots and it's way harsher than I expected. I feign pleasure with the antifreeze running down my throat. I shoot the other one before he can depress me with another alcohol-induced toast.

The night becomes a blur.

🌿   🌿   🌿

At home I slink in, trying not to ruffle the bed, the blankets, the wife.

"What time is it?" she says.

"Late."

"Was it fun?" she mumbles.

"Yes, yes, go back to sleep."

"You drunk?"

"No."

"You drive?"

"Not drunk. Go back to sleep."

"Did Ray drive?"

"Please, baby."

"I smell it," she says, and rolls over. "Boozy. Don't be dangerous."

"Love you, too."

In the quiet I close my eyes. I dream about my wife. We're in a town with no name but we're having a party. We're kissing, the way we do when all else falls away. Ray is there and Katrina is in a wedding dress. My wife wants to kiss again. She loves me. The smell of her skin, the brush of her eyebrows against my cheek. Katrina wants to show me her hands. "Look," she says, "no lifeline. I have no lifeline." Her palms are smooth, like porcelain.

When I wake up my wife is snuggled next to me, her breath against my chest. I kiss her, her nose, her nostrils. I kiss her warm ear. The dream was to remind me that I'm not Ray. I'm just his friend. Because someone has to be. I go to take a piss and it lasts forever. I try to hit the side of the toilet so it's not so loud. And then I hear the front door. It's 3:20 a.m. I walk out of the bedroom and see him in the front hallway. Ray and Lizzie with suitcases and Katrina like a zombie, standing but asleep in her pajamas.

"Where are you going?"

His face is empathetic. "Sorry to wake you, buddy. We got to split."

"What are you talking about? It's three in the morning."

"I'll call you," he says, and shuts the door.

I watch them from the window, Katrina shuffling, brain-dead.

"Idiot." I lift the window a crack. "Leave her with me, Ray! Ray, leave her here for tonight!"

"What is he doing?" my wife says behind me.

"I don't know. He's acting on impulse."

"Stop him."

"I tried," I say. "Katrina's asleep."

"Why would they do this to her?"

"You want me to tackle him?" I ask.

"I hate him," she says. "Okay? Hate that dude."

"Got it."

"Can't be a good parent if you're still a child," she says. "And Lizzie, God."

My wife goes back to bed. I walk into Alex's room and see one of his eyes open. I sit on his bed and grip his ankle beneath the blanket. "You still awake, pal?"

He moves slowly, as if locked in that position for hours. His chin rests on my knee and I'm touched but saddened by his lonesome pain.

"I'm sorry I said you'd probably die before me," he says.

"Oh, that's okay, don't worry about it."

"I think I might need help," he says.

The words find me. I absorb them as shards. The pain is his, I tell myself. He deserves my strength. I think of my mother, my wife, my own days of gray, so many years ago.

"I'll find someone tomorrow," I say. "Someone you can talk to."

I wait for him to speak, to affirm my reading of his words. He nods, and turns to face the wall.

Evolution

nstead of Googling therapists I call my mother. She takes twenty minutes to give me two names in our area and I call both. Dr. Michael Zinnman is a psychologist for teen boys and wrote a book four years ago that sold two million copies. I don't love that he's famous and probably did the *Today* show during his tour. I anticipate an office built to showcase the awards he's accumulated for innovative thinking, complete with a framed photo of him and Regis. The next person is Dr. Judith Hallow. She received her PhD at Harvard, her office is in St. Petersburg, she looks a little like Ruth Buzzi from *Laugh-In*. I'm comforted by the orange cat on the couch behind her and I like the sole candle lit on her desk. Jackie likes the famous doctor and thinks a male might work better for our boy. So we book it.

The three of us meet him at his office, on the fourth floor of a building downtown. We sit in a circle of chairs surrounded by floor plants that block most of his accolades on the wall. The carpet is teal, the windows shut but large. The view is water only, and a piece of the pier. A white-noise machine hums gently in the corner, blocking all quiet truths from the waiting room. Alex is bouncing his left foot with the speed of a rock drummer. I come centimeters from resting my hand on his knee. I stop myself in time. I turn to my wife instead and she smiles, rests her hand on my knee. The doctor is probably in his late fifties with a full head of wavy brown hair and wears a Tampa Bay Rays tie. His aura couldn't be kinder, more approachable, more tender. I want to open up to this man, to tell him that my brother is a self-righteous egomaniac, that I wish I had achieved more career-wise, and that my father was absent enough to prove his lack of interest in loving me. But alas, I'm not here for me. He asks us to start, to give him some background. He addresses Alex with respect and zero pretension. When my son begins to talk, the doctor leans forward and finds his eyes. A soft and palpable empathy leaps from the man's presence—his nodding, the way his teeth come into view with certain changes of expression. I listen to Alex's tone go from inaudible reluctance to something to work with.

"I think there are two kids that like me at school. I think they do. I eat with them, and yes, sometimes we talk on the phone.

No, I haven't called my San Francisco friends. I'm embarrassed about things I did when I lived there and now I don't want to talk to any of those people.

No, I don't want to talk about those things now.

I don't sleep very much. I'm up at night. Thinking about bad stuff. Death, my dad's, mostly, waking up and knowing I'll never see him again. Or my mother's plane crashes on one of her business trips and I can't tell her I miss her because she's dead. I think about sickness, cancer, the disease that eats human flesh, the shrinking of the planet, global warming, starvation, drowning, quicksand, breathing toxins, basketball in phys ed with terrible people that are better than me at sports, Israeli and Arab children killed by misfired Scuds, and so many things I did to embarrass myself when I was younger."

"Jackie," the doctor says.

"Yes?"

"Are you aware of any of the things Alex might have done when he was younger that would be embarrassing for him in hindsight?"

She looks at Alex and his face works as he tries to avoid the pain of his memories.

"One thought I'm having is that Alex used to pretend he was Batman."

My son covers his face with his hand.

"Okay," the doctor says. "How does pretending you were Batman embarrass you, Alex?"

He can't speak; his hand reaches for a leaf from one of the plants.

"There's not one person in the world, Alex, who hasn't done things when they were younger that they feel awkward about now. For example, when I was a kid, I used to dress in my mother's clothes. Not only did I go into her closet and come out looking like a bag lady, but I wanted all my relatives to see me. I'd do this on Thanksgiving," he says and laughs.

We smile and Alex grins to be kind. He looks at me out of the corner of his eye.

"I remember growing older," the doctor continues, "thirteen or so, and I never wanted to see these relatives again, none of them. They'd show up each year hoping to God I'd run into my mother's closet and give them a show. Dancing, singing. I was finished with all that. Never again, so silly and such a stupid thing a younger person would do. I was older now, trying to find my manhood, my role as an individual person, and the last thing I needed was these awful memories of dressing up like an old lady, of all things."

Alex laughs enough to make his shoulders hop. He sees me again. I feel as if the money we're spending on this is the best usage of cash I've ever exhibited. I want to put this guy on a retainer. I want to pay him now, out of pocket. Maybe we can come to this office after school every day, the place where my son smiles at me and even laughs. We're all silent for a moment and I can see the doctor is trying to get Alex to speak, to lead us to the next round of this incredible progress.

In time the doctor says, "Feel like sharing one of the things you did when you were younger that's really awkward to remember now?"

Alex shifts in his seat, unsure if he wants the stage, alone. He reaches again for one of the leaves and begins to bend it. "No, thank you."

The doctor crosses and uncrosses his leg. He blinks; a thought, an idea?

"I have a thought for you. All of you. You moved here from California; Mom is busy at work and Dad is running the show at home. Tell me if I'm wrong, but there's no place to hang out with kids your age if it's not at school."

Alex nods.

"I think it might be time for a party. A welcome to St. Petersburg party. See it as an introduction to all the new people in your lives. What do you think?"

🍂　　🍂　　🍂

We leave with a plan for a pool party. We hear him. A gathering of Alex's peers and their families. The school is so formal and they don't throw parties for the kids. Not on Halloween, not even at

Christmas. It's time to see his classmates out of their private school uniforms. Swim, play volleyball, eat hotdogs and nachos, and see how many memories form from a nice Sunday in the backyard. Jackie and I can't believe we didn't think of it on our own. We have the space, the pool, a yard. We even have a trampoline. I'll serve ribs and baked beans and buy booze because everyone here drinks during the day on weekends and people will stop by. It's a plan.

※　　※　　※

Parents I've never met are loving my margaritas, smiling in ways they hadn't expected, even shifting their hips slightly to the Rolling Stones on my turntable. Alex is hanging out with kids from his class. I see him between hosting, sighing deeply, taking short moments to rub his eyes, to be alone in spurts. The swirl of it all exhausts him. He's really trying. I put my arm around him because I'm buzzing off tequila, forgetting I don't get to hug him anymore, especially in public. He doesn't like it. Doesn't matter. My brain is in a good light. A couple walks in with their son. I recognize the man; he's Alex's science teacher. On back-to-school night he waffled over how to explain the school's unwritten respect for creationism as a viable philosophy for teaching our existence. I remember looking around the room, waiting for the obligatory *hiss* from some liberal parent, any Democrat. But this is the Deep South. Churchgoing is major here; in fact, we met a couple who asked us which church we belonged to before asking us our names. I shake his hand, reintroduce myself, and pull Jackie aside.

"It's the Adam and Eve teacher," I say.

"I know. Be nice."

"Adam and Eve!" I say.

My wife points at my margarita, without a word. This means I'm drinking too much and as a result I might say or think stupid things. But I can't stop staring at him.

"By the way," my wife says, "he never said he was teaching creationism. That's just what you heard."

"Tell me what you heard," I say.

She walks away. Into the kitchen. I know what I heard. The teacher was impressive, a major traveler, Peace Corps, you name it. He's built bridges in Uganda, scaled Kilimanjaro, and once nursed a baby bald eagle to flight after it was hit by a UPS truck. I remember the thrill in his eyes, his obvious gift for teaching. And then his energy changed as the singsongy rhythm of his accomplishments died down.

"When it comes to evolution, we'll *discuss* Darwinian theory." Pause, pause, pause. "With our minds open to all theories of our existence." Pause, pause, pause. "Did I mention the four field trips?"

I think about my kids and their ironed uniforms and tuition. I put the margarita down and get a glass of water. So much effort and money went into their acceptance into a nondenominational school. This man, this living Indiana Jones, is afraid of losing his job, afraid to say that evolution is the actual reason he got into science to begin with. He is passionate about his chosen field, but he must assuage the majority of the paying customers with a nod to church involvement.

My wife says I look like a serial killer. I shake my head to snap out of it.

"Hey, Todd," I bark at some man I recognize. I don't even think the guy's name is Todd. He smiles at me, thinks he knows me, but doesn't know it's my house. He's wearing a forest-green golf shirt, matching shorts, and sneakers with white socks. He carries a short glass of Patrón and his eyes float a bit.

"I hear you're a writer?" he says.

I nod, take a long sip from my water glass. "You want more ribs?"

"I ate nine."

"I got three pounds of coleslaw," I announce with pride, a bounce on my toes.

"So what do you write? Would I know your books?"

"No, no, I wish. I'm just a copywriter, and an editor."

"Got any best sellers?"

I take another long sip, and look at my shoes. "No."

"So what, like, mysteries, stuff like that?"

I don't write mysteries. I look for my wife's head in the crowd. I find myself nodding now, agreeing. "Yes. Mysteries."

He gets me now, yes. Todd is psyched. He just bagged a new friend. One who writes mysteries. This could be very good for Todd, his neighbors seeing us together. They might even think he and I are planning to write a book together. I think of Angela Lansbury when I think of mysteries. A murder in a bed and breakfast on Nantucket. Only the cat saw what really happened. Call Angela Lansbury.

"I don't read much," he says, now chomping on an ice cube.

"Me neither," I say, and he laughs, his large paw on my shoulder.

Todd feels guilt for not being a reader. I see it in his face. But he laughs it off, sticks his tongue out, becomes the expected American sitcom dad. His discomfort comes from his belief that I'm a smarter human than he is. Me being a mystery writer and all. I feel obliged to comfort him, to tell him it's not such a big deal, let's talk about something else.

"Do you golf?" I ask.

"Three hours this morning. You?" he asks.

"A bad one."

Todd sits next to me near the pool. He runs his finger around the rim of his glass and thanks me for the food, the invite, the "really cool" music.

"Glad you're happy, friend."

He gives me a warm look I've seen before. It can be described as: I remember a guy like you in college. It's so nice to be reminded of him. I feel lucky that your type of person is here, with us, and maybe some of you will rub off on me.

"My name is Tom."

I knew it wasn't Todd.

"Nice to meet you," I say.

He extends his hand and wants to take it "jive," our fingers now entangled, his facial expression like Coolidge from *The White Shadow*. I smile at him, wanting him to know he's safe in his attempt to go jive. It's still in you, isn't it, Tom? All that rhythm, all those long-forgotten handshakes from high school. You're still alive, Thomas. There's a twinkle of danger left in you.

"Can I get you another drink?" he asks me.

"Sure," I say. "I'll have a margarita."

He stands and I stop him.

"Hey, Tom?"

"Yeah?"

"You know they're teaching our kids that evolution is just a theory? Implying creationism carries just as much possibility in explaining our existence as Darwinian theory?"

He's staring at me, a slight sway to his large frame, one eyebrow higher than the other.

"You know something?" he says.

"Tell me."

"You look a lot like Gretzky. Wayne Gretzky."

Busted

| *Lightning touches the ground eleven times in eight minutes*

My wife has a one-night trip to New York for work. We consider the idea of my joining her. I start to see it. The slick hotel room with those Egyptian sheets and art deco lamps that don't have chains or on/off switches. Digital flat-screen TV, room service, uninhibited sex, and probably a terrycloth robe with the hotel insignia sewn in. Tara could sleep at Ginger's house if Teri says okay. Alex could maybe stay alone. Alone? Maybe he could call Ryan, the buddy he mentions from time to time. I'll talk to him.

Tara's bedtime. The fish tank awaits. We're reading *Charlie and the Chocolate Factory* and I'm not sure it's the best read for a girl who has nightmares.

""'Augustus," his mother screams. "Get him out! He'll be killed!"' Okay, let's stop for tonight."

"Don't stop, Daddy; he's still in the tube."

"Let's go to bed."

"Fine. Closets."

I check and re-close her folding closet doors.

"Under."

I used to get on my knees to glance underneath her bed. Now I just motion that way and it suffices. "Nothing under there." I kiss her.

"Ladybug."

My son gets another hour to be the oldest, to stay up. I find him in his bed with his giant headphones on at 10:30 p.m. The glow of the film *Ted* lights his sagging eyes.

"Ready for bed, pal?"

"Five more minutes."

"Five more, okay? Then lights out."

I sit on the end of his bed and he waits for me to speak. He removes one of the ears of his headphones.

"Got a question for you," I say.

"Okay."

"Mom has a trip to New York on Friday and I was thinking of joining her. It would be one night and we were wondering if you wanted to invite Ryan over or maybe consider going to his house for the evening."

He stares at me and slowly removes the other earbud. "You're both leaving?"

"That was the idea, but just for a night. Feel like calling Ryan and . . . ?"

"No, no."

"Why not?"

"I just want to stay here."

"Okay. Ryan could sleep here, you guys could order pizza, watch movies. I'll get the first plane back and be home early."

He leans back on his pillow and his head rolls to the side. He's seeing the entire scenario in his head and I'm waiting to see how it plays out for him. After three full minutes I have my answer. I kiss him, a no-no, but I do it anyway.

"Forget what I said," I say. "I'll stay home."

My wife walks in and kisses us both. My phone rings and I leave the room to answer it. I can hear only breathing on the other end, a pocket dial, maybe.

"Dude, you there?" a man's voice says.

"Yes, hello?" I say. It's Ray.

It appears Ray and Lizzie had a fight and broke up. Three days afterward, Ray dropped Katrina off at Lizzie's sister's place. Ray is quite hated by Lizzie's sister Maureen, and Maureen and her boyfriend, Will, nearly came to blows with Ray while Katrina ran upstairs amid a barrage of curse words and chest thumping. In the vaguely recalled seconds in which Ray exited the premises, he may or may not have kicked the screen door to Maureen's back porch. Ray returned to his home, he explains to me in the tone of an altar boy. He says he showered (really?), shaved (come on, you did not shave), and sat down for dinner, alone. In his version, he's eating a Hungry-Man frozen dinner, obviously the only meal he could think of quickly, the only meal he could feasibly make for himself. Anyway, not long after Mr. Sunshine goes to bed, the cops are at his door. They have a warrant for his arrest; the words *battery* and *home invasion* are used as his rights are read; his hands are cuffed. He is taken, according to him, into the street in his boxer shorts.

"Please come and bail me out. I'll pay you back with interest. My mother's not answering her phone and my father said he doesn't have the money. Please, brother. I could really use a friend."

My wife is still in Alex's room. Tara snores lightly across the hall. Jackie and I go to the den and turn on Jon Stewart.

"Who was on the phone?" she says.

"I have to go to New Jersey," I say.

My wife turns the TV off and faces me.

"Ray's been arrested. His father won't bail him out."

She shakes her head, ready to tell me she "knew this would happen." She swallows the thought, recognizing it would irritate me.

"Why can't one of the other guys take care of him?"

"He called me."

"He doesn't have Michael's number?"

"Michael's out of town."

"What about Nick?"

I shake my head but she doesn't see.

"It'll all work out," I say. "His father won't or *can't* get him out. Let me help him. He's sitting in there with who knows who."

"Ugh, this guy. I'm sorry," she says. I feel her hand on my shoulder. "You're right. He's a friend and he needs you."

"It's maddening, I know."

"I'm being selfish, I guess," she says.

"I'd hope he'd come help me."

"*I'd* help you."

"Right. But not if you were traveling."

"That hurts."

"Kidding."

"No, you're not."

"I know you'd help me."

Jon Stewart is speaking directly to us but the TV is muted. My wife turns him off and nuzzles-up to me. "Want to try to have a baby?"

"Not right now," I say.

She turns *The Daily Show* back on, this time with sound. I can't tell if she's upset.

After five minutes I shake her. She's asleep.

I take the remote control. I flick the channel, again and again, and land on *The Golden Girls*. It's a marathon on channel 1496. Ray is in jail. My wife wants a third child. My son is in therapy. I settle into the couch. Bea Arthur is telling it like it is. I should write about the elderly, the human alchemy of bracing to die. These ladies are hilarious, the sitcom written so well. There's a building cadence in the dialogue, each of them chiming in until the crest is found, a self-deprecating yet surprisingly witty snippet of geriatric truth. I find #79 and write *geriatric jungle gym*. I shut the book and hear the final guffaw of the laugh-track button. Applause.

Elite

| *Seventy-six degrees in the a.m., the moon visible, the sun so low*

"We're ready. We're now ready to board our Elite, Gold, and Silver members. I repeat, our Elite, Gold, and Silver members only at this time, please."

The airline employee speaking to us is named Beverly. Her tone suggests she too is a member of an elite group of well-uniformed staffers, trained to get the wealthy and coiffed on the plane before us scumbags. Does anyone but me see the hypocrisy in using the language of class hierarchy when your airplanes are thirty years old? I mean, the toilet seats are brown and cracked from thousands upon thousands of asses. On my way down the ramp I see patched bolt panels in the wing of the plane. A quick fix, if you will. Antiquated is the kindest euphemism one can use in describing something you've chosen to hand your life over to.

In my seat I take out #79 and write the words *Bail out Ray. Serotonin. Rank toilet seat.* I tell myself not to order a drink because I fall asleep on planes without trying. I think it's the steady hum. Like being lulled by embryonic fluid. Fast machine, so many people on board, including babies and nuns. I order a water. I take two sips and I'm asleep. Within a half hour my underwear is suddenly soaked through, the water spilled. Some air pocket beneath my testicles makes me feel as though there's a quarry of even colder water underneath. I'm a child and I've wet myself. The woman next to me pretends she saw none of it. I stretch the wet denim and slink off to the bathroom.

New Jersey is ready for me. In full bustle, Newark Airport reminds me that Florida is an idyllic vacation land of cocoa butter and chlorine. This is where I'm from, but I feel lost to the rhythm expected of me here, so close to New York. I've been gone so long, I could be Amish. Look at this cruel world where rainwater is black from spinning tires and billowy plumes of smoke rise from industrial chimneys. The cab driver's radio is blasting a local talk show channel and the news is read in a machine-gun monotone.

"Two dead in fire at 161st Street in Manhattan; Police say a basement explosion is to blame. Found in the home was an infant now in custody. The owner of the building is yet to be found."

I couldn't be more sad for this child.

"Yankees lose, Mets win; G. W. Bridge is a parking lot. Traffic at the top of the hour on Ten-Ten Wins."

I dial Ray and he picks up on the first ring. "Hey, my dad bailed me out."

"He what? I mean, good, good. You're out."

"I'm at home. You here?"

"Yes, Ray. You said your dad couldn't afford it."

"I guess he found it. Got guilty. Thanks for coming," he says softly.

"Well, you don't need me now."

"I need you, come over."

"I should head back, man. I came to get your ass out of . . ."

"Please, come to my house," he says and hangs up.

I arrive at Ray's house in South Orange. Katrina answers the door and I lift her into my arms. I hug her as if she's my own, squeezing, connecting, assuaging all the thoughts I've had about her since they left so abruptly. I even get a kiss. Ray's mother is behind her. Katrina calls her Ta Ta but I'm not sure why. The house smells like boiled meat and old sofas.

I see Ray in the kitchen, sitting over a bowl of rice, a cigarette freshly lit for my arrival. He wants me to know he's deeper now, having been in the clink. I begin to hate him already.

"So happy you're here," he says, standing to receive his embrace.

"Not sure you need me."

"Of course I do," he says, wide-eyed, pulling me into the living room to see a taped, broken window. "She threw a rock through it."

"Lizzie?"

"Of course. Look at it."

It's actually a brick.

"She threw that at your window?"

"She's a horrific, insensitive, naive . . ."

I look over at Katrina and her oblivious grandmother. "I got it, Ray," I tell him. "I don't need to hear her whole resume."

Ta Ta approaches. Somehow she was old when I knew her in 1984. Grayish, unkempt hair, a robe during the day. Always the smell of black coffee, of a human just awakened from bed. Ray has three older siblings. I think his mother had him when she was in her mid to late forties.

"How come you don't age?" she asks me and reaches for my longish hair.

"We're all aging," I say.

"We sure are."

Ray points at the shattered glass on the carpet, as if the brick isn't enough evidence. "Look at this," he says, kneeling to pick it up. "Crazy bitch had me arrested for nothing, nothing!" He stands with the glass and dumps it in an ashtray, shaking his head. He takes a long dramatic pull off the cigarette like he's Columbo.

"What's important is you're out," I say to the room.

"I know," he says. "I had a kid with that maniac. Why didn't you stop me from even touching that skank?"

Katrina is sitting on the floor with her notebook and her big pencil. She looks at me before hovering over the book, her chin nearly touching the paper.

"You want a beer or something?" Ray asks.

"No, thanks."

"So, anyway, thank God I'm out. I'm thinking of calling the cops about the brick. Liz is in so much trouble, man." A drag off his cigarette.

"I'm going to do some writing with Katrina. You think you could smoke that in the kitchen?"

He looks down at the cigarette in his hand. "Sorry, sorry," he says, exhaling in a stream as he goes.

I remove #79 from my bag and get down on the floor. Katrina is trying not to smile. Her lips are pursed together, her reddish hair tossing from side to side as she reads her last sentence to me.

"Moo-moo didn't have anyone to take him to the party so he bought his own tuxedo at the mall. Parking was murder so he pulled into the tuxedo store and parked beneath all the cummerbunds."

Katrina's head lifts for a reaction. I point at her, smiling. "You're a writer, girl."

"Thank you. Your turn, you start."

"Sounds good."

The tuxedo felt too snug. And for some reason the bow tie was yellow and the jacket was green and the slacks were flannel and the cummerbund was made of extra-lean ground sirloin.

Ray pokes his head in the room. "It's her," he says. "Your mother wants you on the phone."

Katrina, silent but defiant, begins to write again. Her face is stern, the pencil pressing into the paper.

"Did you hear me, Katrina?"

She doesn't budge, just writes harder and harder until the pencil tip snaps. "I hate her!" Katrina screams and runs past Ray and up the stairs.

Ray lets out a long and miserable sigh. "I do too but she's your mother and you got to talk to her."

"*No!*" she screams from upstairs. Door *SLAM*.

I get up from the floor and sit on the couch.

"She doesn't want to talk to you, Liz. She ran upstairs crying."

He looks at me as Lizzie speaks on the other end.

"Yeah, yeah, tell me all about it!" he yells. "You had me arrested for nothing, you bitch. I spent the night in a cell with a mass *murderer,* okay? Some mother you turned out to be! Watch your back, you effing *witch!*"

He slams the phone down hard, once, twice, three times. It must be smashed to bits. I'm almost sure I heard flesh too, his finger or hand between the phone and cradle. When I step inside he's holding all five fingers as if he'd caught them in a car door. He can't breathe. Man, he's having a tough day.

"Let me see it."

"No! She wants me to die in pain."

"She's not being nice right now."

"She'll take Katrina away from me and treat her like shit."

"We won't let her."

"She'll grow up to be the same woman. A lame and soggy townie."

"We owe the world better."

"I hate her."

"Can I see your hand?" I ask.

His right middle finger looks broken. Raised purple knuckle; the way he holds it, quivering. He looks down at it. "Oh, man." He attempts to pull a cigarette out of the package. It drops. I watch him go down to his knees to retrieve it. He tries to light it down there.

"*Raaaaay!*" his mother screeches. "Katrina's cryin'. Go talk to her!"

Ray stands and walks away.

"Bye," I say to no one and decide to leave. I walk down the block and make a right on Raymond Street. I walk through town and to the train station. I look at the schedule and eventually get on a 3:45 to Penn Station. From there I get a bus to Newark Airport and pay a hundred dollars to switch my flight to one that leaves in an hour. I arrive in Tampa by 10:00 p.m.

I kiss my wife's cheek but she doesn't budge. Everyone's asleep. I'm not tired yet. The mail is in a pile and I open a letter addressed to me. It's from my brother's wife. An invitation to join them for Cam's fiftieth birthday party. Two airline tickets included; wipes out the possibility of an excuse to bail. My brother and I clash over money. He believes I have none and will never make any. Money is his drug of choice. On the answering machine are my mother, my father-in-law, Ray, and Dr. Zinnman.

My mother: "Hi, wondering if you're coming up for Cam's birthday. But more importantly, I have to tell you about this new ginger root. Its sole purpose is to introduce flailing serotonin to available receptors. I know Alex is particular about what he eats but there are many ways to doctor up the taste and make it edible. I'm excited. Call me."

My father-in-law: "Hi Jackie, just wanted you to know it's Mom's birthday tomorrow, so I'm drinking a 1990 Barolo. Miss you, love you. Looking forward to visiting."

Ray: "Dude, did you leave? Just like that? Did you just walk out the door and go home? Are you a dick or what? My hand isn't broken. Hurts though. I can't believe you left. Katrina was asking where you went. Dick."

Alex's doctor: "Hi, Jackie and Jay. Can you give me a call? I want to discuss a few things in regard to Alex and holistic medication."

He wants to medicate my son. His tone is dark, so unlike his normal air. It's as if he's bracing for the hardest part of his job: telling the parents that their son would be better off medicated. I lie on the couch, hearing the doctor's words, and fall asleep. I dream of a marinating brain. It floats in a mason jar filled with thick white sauce. I dip my finger in the vat. I touch the tip to my tongue.

Elite 2

Ninety-nine degrees at 8:00 a.m; the driveway pavement bends and bakes

We decide Alex could use a break from school. Just one day. I'll take him to Cam's birthday party, show him Times Square. He's been there but only a few times. I'm excited to tell him.

"No, thanks," he says.

"It'll be fun. Just you and me. You can skip school."

"I don't like New York so much."

"You haven't been there in years."

"But I remember thinking it was awful. Loud and crowded. No thanks."

So I force him to go.

He's not saying much on the plane but his earbuds are in. At least there's some music in his world. I break out the holistic meds Dr. Zinnman suggested. St. John's wort. He'll take two a day on a full stomach and we'll see if his mood and energy and ability to sleep improve. He holds the pill and stares at it. Let's Google it. *Hypericum perforatum.* Also known as rosin rose, chase-devil, and goatweed. Ranked higher than the placebo in studies regarding the remedy of mood swings and low serotonin. All natural. I watch him take it and wait for it to work. Nothing so far. He pushes his earbuds deeper and rests his head on the window.

Our hotel is three blocks from my brother's place in Greenwich Village. The decor is très minimalist so the one chair has a bicycle seat. The TV is cool. Huge. Alex turns it on and gets under his covers. I can see only his eyes, the top of his head.

"Don't get too comfy, buddy, we gotta get some lunch. Let's go up to Times Square."

"Why?"

"Oh man, wait until you see it. The energy, the color of it all."

"I kind of like it here," he says, changing the channel.

"But New York awaits. It's electric, just listen to it. Hear that?"

"Yes, I hear a lot of things out there."

"We have to have dinner with your uncle Cam in three hours, so let's go get some lunch so we can come back, shower, and head off. Your first cousin is coming to dinner too. Remember her? Kimmy? You used to call her Baby Kimmy?"

His eyes close before he lifts the blanket over his face. I shake his right foot. Nothing. "You comin'?"

"Okay. Okay already."

The restaurant is in the heart of Times Square. A themed eatery. I thought it might be fun to dine among Dracula and Frankenstein, have a waiter in werewolf garb. How often do you get to be among real actors as you eat? We stand on a half-mile line; the crowd is cranky, hungry, going nowhere with clunky bags and coats. A man dressed as a mummy walks by and asks how many our party will be.

I tell him two and he writes it down. I want to ask him what the holdup is but I feel stupid. Asking a mummy how long. Alex could be standing anywhere. His facial expression suggests there's no reason to be here, no need to engulf ourselves in this sticky-tired milieu of tourists. A child weeps, a cell phone rings, a woman dressed as Elvira says, "Goldfarb, party of six, follow me . . . or else!"

"This is awful," Alex mumbles.

I pat his lower back. "Soon, soon," I pray. On the walls are fake portraits of ghostly men, whose mouths move as they announce the lunch specials: "Todaaaaay we have Cornish game hens stuffed with rosemary and garlic."

"Oooh," says a vampire voice. "Please, no garlic!"

A family gets on line behind us. The father is yelling at both his kids. "We tried the Hard Rock, didn't we? We were there, it was a zoo. We're eating here and that's goddamn final!"

The mummy walks up to them and asks, "How many?" The daughter screams, I mean screams, like in a horror movie. The mummy blinks twice and repeats, "How many in your party?"

"Four," the father says. "How long, how long till we sit?"

"Hopefully not an eternity," the mummy says, and leaves.

The man and I have eye contact but I look away. He is not happy.

"I don't feel so well," Alex says, and I think of the pill, the St. John's wort. "Can we leave? Just go back to the hotel. I'm not that hungry anyway."

I'm hungry. That's the only reason I'm still standing here. A dry ice machine is triggered; I see the plume coming right at us. A man dressed as a hunchback emerges from the fog and hands us each phones that will vibrate when our table is ready. I hand the thing to the furious guy behind me and Alex and I reenter New

York City. I get a cab and within a half hour my son is back under the covers and flicking channels. We call for room service, club sandwiches and fries, and I find out where tonight's restaurant is located. It's right next to Cam's apartment. We could get dressed a little early and go surprise him. He hasn't seen Alex since last Thanksgiving at my mom's.

My son's eyelids are half open. I get under the covers in my bed and pull the blanket to my nose. I hear the horns outside, the cabs, the bustle. What if we just stayed here and never left? I watch TV and drift, sensing the tingle of nap time rising. My pillow so feathery, my feet still in socks. I wake up with an hour to get to the restaurant. I'm up, showering, drying off, calling out to Alex, "We gotta go, man." When I check on him, all I see is a sleeping lump.

"Alex, let's go, we're going to be late for Uncle Cam's dinner."

He doesn't budge.

I pull my pants on and shake his bed with my foot. "Let's go, buddy!"

"I want to stay here."

"No, no. We came all this way to see family. Come on, blankets off, grab some clothes."

He throws the blanket off. "Fuck this!" he yells.

"What's wrong?"

"I don't like it here. I don't want to go. I don't like being out there. I never liked New York."

"It's exciting."

"I told you I hated it."

"You can't *hate* New York."

"Why not? It's loud and has no order. I don't like it."

"You don't really know it. There's an energy."

"I *hate* the energy. Just let me stay here. I'll feel better if I just stay here."

I sit on the end of the bed and stare at him. The right thing to do. Call his mother? See if she can get him out of bed?

"Alex?"

"What?"

"I'm trying to say and do the right thing here, buddy. But there's also part of me that wants to just grab you and say, *this* is life, *this* is a moment and we're here and it's *so* different from your normal life. Maybe you'd thank me if I made you come, told you I'm your father and this is the decision we're making tonight."

He sits up quickly, the blanket falling to his chest. "I'm telling you how I feel. You can ignore me, but I'm telling you how I feel."

"And I was excited about showing you New York."

"You didn't ask me, you just took me here."

"Let's go to dinner, Alex."

"I don't feel well. I started a new medication and I don't feel well."

I look down at my hands and my fingers are clasped. I leave the hotel alone. I won't apologize. To any of these people. He's a teen and he's fried. Not my fault. Text him. Not me. Tell *him* that you're disappointed. Not me. I'm fifteen minutes early so I walk into a bar next to the restaurant. The martini I choose is a Bombay Sapphire. I take out #79 and write, *I'm not a fascist father who barks at his kid when it's time to be heard.* I take a long deep breath and recognize where I am. The exaggerated sounds of the city belong to me, my memory. Bursts of cab horns, the squeal of an overstuffed truck. I look outside and see a spurt of gray smoke from a manhole. A man in a suit walks through the cloud, his briefcase swinging, his eyebrows defiant. Does he think he's being filmed?

Into the bar comes a tall man. I name him Larry. He kisses the cheek of the lady making drinks and settles onto the stool next to mine. There are fourteen or more other choices but I guess he likes me and needs our shoulders to touch. I scoot over one and he eyes me, wondering why I'm being so distant, in Manhattan. The lady asks him what he wants. He sighs and prepares a line. "As long as it's cold and tastes like Heineken, I'll take two."

He went with slick, over funny.

He sips from each and goes into a story about himself and "dis girl I'm after who told Jimmy I look like Pacino. So I tell her I'm single but that I like Doreen, a friend of hers. Oh man does she get all jealous in her eyes, ya know, and I'm like, you don't own me."

I think about the lonely. Talking in lies, just to impress a woman paid to listen. He is a dime a dozen. God forgot about him, produced him in a package deal where instead of being built as an individual he came in a satchel of ten men who look and act and eat and sleep and marry and die the same way. It's worrisome that I might be a part of this package. The bartender nods, takes a moment between customers to tend to herself, rubbing her eyes, refolding her bar rag.

"I can't exactly afford two girlfriends," says Larry, sensing the disinterest. He laughs to himself, finishes the first Heineken.

In my notebook I write as much of the dialogue as I can remember. I'll give Larry an apartment in Canarsie. And Mets tickets. He also loves cheese steak. Yellow American cheese only.

It's time to see my brother.

Cam was born in September, almost five years earlier than I. At fourteen he began loathing my presence, my face, my scent, the way my mother and I connected. His face during a temper tantrum consisted of a violent underbite and the squinting eyes of an escaped killer. He punched hard, mostly into my leg, just below my butt. But I remember his words most. The machine-gun quips about my lack of worthiness would stick to me forever. I began to consciously skirt him, to leave a room he was entering, to keep quiet so as not to feed his need to deflate or belittle me. I've employed this technique well into adulthood. My memories of the way he kept me timid, even afraid, as a kid are too vivid for anyone's good. I justify these thoughts as fodder for writing I haven't done, may never do. Because the notion of publishing truths about my brother Cam is about as awkward as telling him what he already knows: he's an asshole.

My mother used to explain his taunting and acerbic antagonism as a "glitch in his connectivity." She said such things in an attempt to produce empathy in me for him. Cam spent almost the full first month after his birth with only sporadic visits from my mother. The story goes that Mom caught a virus during her cesarean that kept her doped up and bedridden for twenty-three days. The result? Lunatic boy. I have a memory of him kicking our babysitter in the ass, hard, after she turned the TV off and told him to go to bed. In high school he broke into a morgue with his friends and brought a human hand to a party. My mother hired a shrink. After a few therapy sessions Cam left town in a used Honda Accord with a girl named Lisa, whose parents called the police. They were both retrieved from a motel on Route 22 but Cam left again the following weekend, this time alone. He ended up in San Diego. He was seventeen.

Today he is one of the top five builders of low-income "mirror" housing in southern California and one of the top investors in Oracle. Over ten years ago he made his first million and two years later was in a group photograph of "up-and-comers" in *Fortune* magazine. I've spent so many hours in my head, praying he'd be humbled by a financial tsunami, anything to correct his karma. But the man never got as much as a paper cut. He just kept winning and getting tanner and smelling more exotic when I would see him at my mom's house on Thanksgiving. Today he's worth $50 million or more and I know this because my mother sends me articles about him. The guy burned every bridge he ever crossed and giggled when he got to the other side. Most people, overtly or quietly pay for their mistakes, their innate insensitivities to humankind. Not my brother. He's immune to backlash.

The restaurant is small, Italian. It gives off a warm, antique light into the street. I see Cam in the back. I walk to him and his arms widen. Gordon Gekko. The slicked-back hair, the Armani or Prada suit that shimmers, silver. He's two inches taller than I am and smells like the lobby of the Ritz. He straightens the straight collar of my shirt and takes my cheeks in his hands.

"Where's your son?"

"He wasn't feeling great."

"I fly his little ass all the way up here and he stays in the hotel?"

"I'll pay you back."

"I don't want your money."

"Teens," I say. "Ya know."

"Kimmy is going to be so sad."

"I know, I tried, he's really under the weather. Bad timing, I guess."

"Well, okay, *whatever*, as they say. How's the most incredible brother in the world?" he says.

A very kind sentence for him. He's overcompensating. I'll take it.

"That's so nice to hear," I say.

"Come over, join us. You like oysters?"

"Sometimes."

"Come on, it's New York City, I want you to eat like a king."

"Okay."

"You look worn out."

"I'm fine."

"You look like Keith Richards."

"Why? My hair?" I tousle it.

"Like you're on heroin."

"I'm not on heroin."

"Why are you so tired?" He leans in to whisper. "That wife of yours too busy to blow ya?"

Oh, right. My brother has no interior editor. Somehow he enjoys the shock, the change in the chemistry, an awkward turn. Notice here: he's asked only if my wife has blown me, not how she is or what she's been doing at work, a topic that competes with his financial worth, his only gauge of humans. I'll never, in my entire life, make half the money he's made. Not a quarter. Not a tenth. And this is the sole litmus test he uses to assess me. My wife on the other hand makes real money. This makes him bonkers, that the dough she earns belongs to me too. How could it? How could any bottom-feeder be so lucky?

He laughs. I stare at him, glance at his daughter, Kim, his wife, Kate, both now in earshot.

"Kimmy," I say and hug her. I also hug my sister-in-law, who is on the phone but hangs up for me.

"Look who it is," she says and wraps me in her arms. All of Kate's age is in her face and the skin of her elbows. She has the toned body of a thirty-year-old, blue-black hair, sharp heels, lots of jewelry, educated in England, works for the Hearst Group, is always running, looking back as she does so, apologizing all the while. She asks about the kids, my wife, my copywriting, Florida, our house, our weather, missing San Francisco, private school, my wife's job, and whether or not I know my mother has a plantar wart on the ball of her left foot.

"Good, fine, same, yes, no, good, sorta, expensive, going well. A wart on her foot?"

"Are you hungry?" she asks.

I nod like an eight-year-old.

The age difference between my brother and me means Kate was a grown woman while I was still a kid. I remember wanting her to like me, to see that I could be a great little brother. Before they got so rich she was easier to be around. There was a legitimacy to the connection we had; it wasn't hurried or staged. But time and money and the clothes she chooses to wear have changed her over the years. It's okay to be highbrow and distant if all your friends are the same way, I guess. But there's an unmistakable surfaceness in the air. It's in the way they move, speak, and especially listen. Somehow the coldness is careful, as if time is currency and my allotted minutes are forever waning.

A waiter approaches and my brother is whispering in his ear. The man, Jonathan, is nodding, now rubbing my brother's back. They smile deeply at each other and I envy their closeness.

Kimmy has gorgeous brown hair. I reach to touch it. "You are one beautiful girl," I tell her. "So sorry Alex wasn't feeling well. You'll see him tomorrow."

She straightens her silverware. "Do you live on the beach?" she asks.

"No, but near it."

"Do you ever see dolphins?"

"All the time."

"Really?"

"Yup."

"How about whales?"

"Nope, only at SeaWorld."

"I mean in the wild," Kimmy says.

"No, I've never seen a whale in the wild."

"I have," my brother says, ending his love-fest with Jonathan. "Sitka, Alaska, 1983."

"Really?" Kimmy asks. "Orcas?"

"Yes, orcas, a dozen of 'em."

"You never told me that," she says.

"Should've. It was magical."

"Did you take pictures?" she asks.

He shakes his head. "I wish."

"You should all come visit us in Florida," I offer, and take a sip of my water.

"Yes," Cam says, and glances at his wife. "We really do need to get the cousins together. But alas, Alex is not feeling well."

"I agree," Kate says, the glow of her phone lighting her deep crow's feet. "Definitely. We'll get it on the calendar. You gonna have spaghetti, Kimmy? Or do you want the jumbo shrimp again?"

The fact that the discussion about visiting has ended is blatant. There won't be any calendar checking. It smarts only because of their ease in dismissing it all, the idea of watching their daughter interact with mine.

"I guess the shrimp," Kimmy says.

"Everybody know what they want?" Cam asks. "Jonathan is here; we may as well dive in."

"Yes," Kate says.

"Put that menu down," Cam says to me. "You're having oysters with me. You'll love the mahimahi, on a bed of wild rice and asparagus. We'll start with oysters, yes?"

"I don't want oysters," I say, but only to regain my right to order my own dinner. I'm forty-five years old.

He freezes, his hands in the air. "What do you mean? Why not? The fish is religious."

Jonathan walks to my end of the table. My brother introduces me. "He's from Florida but don't hold it against him. He came to the popular conclusion that he wasn't smart enough for New York or pretty enough for Los Angeles so he flew straight for Florida." They laugh, Jonathan laughs. There are so many places I'd rather be.

"We need oysters! Got any Blue Points?"

Jonathan describes what he has, what he wishes he had, and what he has special for my brother. We decide we need more time.

Kimmy rests her head on my shoulder and my whole mood changes.

Kate lowers her eyes to the glowing phone on her lap. "Sorry, so much going on at the office."

"Do what you have to do," I say. She hurries to type and apologetically crams the phone in her purse.

"Okay," she says. "You have my full attention. So tell me about you."

"Really? Do I have to?"

"Yes, what are you up to?"

"The great American novel?" Cam says.

"I wish. I've been adjusting to the new house and taking care of all the logistics. I have been writing," I say, lifting and dropping #79.

"You should pump out a vampire novel," Cam says.

"No, zombies are better now," Kimmy says.

"Fine, zombies. Zombies that live in Malibu."

"I liked Twilight," Kimmy says. "The movie was good too."

"Write one of those," Cam says. "How hard could it be?"

"It's tougher than you think," I say. "You might not realize what it takes to sit there alone for so long with a blank page."

"Oh, bullshit. It's all a formula. I hear Danielle Steel can write a full novel in seven days."

"Well, there you have it then, Cam. Maybe you should give it a try."

"Not me, man. I'm too busy actually working." Cam leans back in his chair. "Not a whole lot of dillydally hours in my day. Never have been. Maybe one day, when I retire and have all the free time in the world."

It's one of the buttons he pushes. Subtly suggesting I have no obligations.

"You're right," I say. "All I do is dillydally."

"Didn't say that," he says. "Said I have to make money during the day or we starve."

"I think you'd be surprised how busy I can be," I say.

He blinks a lot, aims to cross-examine. "What did you make this year?"

"Okay, boys, I don't want to talk about money," says Kate.

Jonathan is back. He holds a bottle of wine out to my brother but Cam doesn't see it. He sees only me. "What did you clear last year after taxes?"

"Sir?" Jonathan says.

My brother glances at the bottle and waves his hand. Jonathan's become more of a servant than a friend. He begins to open the wine.

"Can I have spaghetti and meatballs, please?" Kim says.

"I thought you said you were getting shrimp," her mother says.

"I changed my mind."

"I'll have the same," I say.

"Wait, wait, wait," Cam says. "I thought you were having the fish? It's a two-person meal, man. You have to try it, it's religious." "If it's okay with you, Cam," I say, "just . . . spaghetti and meatballs, please. No oysters for me."

"Great, just great," Cam says. "You don't want 'em means more for me." He glances up at the waiter and lets out a widemouthed laugh. "Bring a dozen, Jonathan. A dozen of the Blue Points." He rubs his hands together and claps. Kimmy flinches. "I bet you fold," he says, pointing at me with his chin. "When you see these babies on ice, you will definitely give in to the pressure."

Yes. Give in to it. The pressure.

"So, Jay," says Kate. "The last time I talked to Jackie, she said you were considering another baby."

Shocked, yes, that my wife even talks to Kate on the phone. I lift a piece of bread and rip it in half. "Really? I hadn't heard that."

I get a laugh from both Kate and Kimmy. My brother has Jonathan's elbow in his clutch, another whisper. My sister-in-law waits for more, even moving the candle on the table to see me better.

"I think it's far-fetched," I say.

"What do you mean?" she asks, wrinkling her forehead.

"That I really don't . . ."

"Cam and Kate!" a woman says. "Look who it is, Charles!"

The man's jaw drops. "Wow, been a while. Is that really you?"

They're old friends but it's been months since they've bumped into each other. Cam stands, Kate stands, the hugging, the kissing, an introduction, this is my younger brother, Jay. They want to sit with us. The man wants to share the oysters with Cam. I envision being teleported out of the restaurant, back to my hotel room. Alex is a genius for skipping this.

"He's from Florida," Cam tells his friend. "But don't hold it against him. He came to the popular conclusion that he wasn't smart enough for New York or pretty enough for Los Angeles so he flew straight for Florida."

Charles likes this quip.

I smile. "Hi," I say, and wave to the guy.

The couple sits. I get Charles next to me. "What do you do, Jay?" he says, and touches my knife and fork.

※　　　※　　　※

Alex is still under the blanket when I get back to the hotel. I sit on my bed and shut my eyes. My brother was built to lean on my buttons.

"How was your night?" I ask.

"Good."

"You hungry?"

"No."

The TV is loud, a commercial for cereal, a tractor, a farm, all that grain.

"You know, Alex, tonight would've been better with you there. I say that because my brother is a giant *dick* and I wanted to have someone in my corner."

He looks at me, hears me.

"I don't want you to feel guilty though."

"Then why do I?" he says.

I smile at him. "Maybe I wanted you to be there for me this time. Life is always going to require sacrifices. We do things for people we love sometimes."

He lifts the blanket higher. "I feel guilty, okay?"

"Why should I have to bend over backwards for that idiot?"

"What?!"

"Not you."

"Get *off* my back! Just get *off*."

The cereal commercial ends and another one comes on for foot fungus cream. I watch the cartoon fungus-man attack a fireman's big toe. He uses a pitchfork.

"I'm sorry," I say. "You're right."

By the time Jon Stewart comes on, we haven't spoken in an hour. My wife calls my cell phone and talks to Alex. He's huddled in the corner, speaking with his hand over his mouth. I'm relieved he has Jackie as an outlet. I wish he could talk to me. He uncoils and hands me the phone.

"Hi," I say.

"Hi," she says. "He's overwhelmed."

"Yeah, I see that."

"Can you be sympathetic?"

"Of course I'm sympathetic."

"He says you got heated, mentioned sacrifices."

"Heated?"

"Did you mention sacrifice?"

"Yes, but not in a way that was rude. We came here for relatives, his cousin."

"He wants to come home."

Alex's phone buzzes. I see his hand slink out from his blanket. It grabs the device from the floor, and drags it back under.

"I don't want him to feel overwhelmed," she says. "It's not the time to test him."

"Okay."

"I want him home, Jay."

"My mother's coming to the party. I told her I'd be there."

"Don't you think your mother wants what's best for Alex?"

His hand exits the blanket, sets the phone back on the floor. I sit on the end of his bed. He doesn't come out from his shell. I bounce twice. Nothing.

"You want to go home, Alex?" I ask him.

"Okay," he says.

"Did he answer you?" my wife says.

Yes. He said he wants to explore the East Village for a few hours, hear some live music and buy a hookah before getting some lunch at a corner spot with brick-oven pizza.

"He says he's ready to come home," I say. "We'll see you tomorrow."

PART TWO

Food for Thought

| *The lawn grew seven inches in a week*

My daughter became a vegetarian for eleven weeks ending last Tuesday. Chicken on the burrito is brand new. I care about her eating meat because I know she'll be less hungry at night if she has something substantial. Otherwise she'll graze and get cranky, I've seen it firsthand. I make one for Alex too. He likes some salsa, a tiny bit of sour cream, but wants the tortilla left open.

Shit, I just put shredded cheese on Tara's wrap. It's too late.

"I hate cheese in my burrito," she says.

"It's a burrito," I say, "right? Shredded cheese is crucial. It's not really a burrito without it."

"I hate cheese on it."

"Just try it."

"Not on burritos," she says.

"Yes, my love, it's good."

"I didn't like it last time."

"You did, you ate it all."

"I was probably starving."

"Just a little cheese."

"Just take it off, Dad. Please."

"Okay, okay."

"Are you mad?" she says.

"Mad about what? Picking shredded cheese from a burrito? That's absurd."

I am mad. Jesus, pick it out yourself, you brat.

"Wait, is this a whole wheat tortilla?" she says.

"Nope."

She bends to sniff the tortilla. I hear the sniff, wait for the reaction. "I don't like the whole wheat kind."

"Hi, all," my wife says, walking in the house. We all face her. "I have a surprise!"

Please let it be flour tortillas.

My wife points, and her father walks in the house with his hands in the air.

"Grandpa's here!" he yells, and Tara runs to him, hugs him, rolls for a moment in the sweet giddiness of their love for each other. I stay back and absorb it all, gaining silently in the richness of familial heart and soul. My father-in-law's visits are great for me. Aside from my happiness at seeing my kids be innately loving, I really like this man and his company. Being alone all day is for the birds. Now, while the wife's at work, he and I will have lunch, take walks along the water, shop for dinner, and watch movies on TV. Of course, he's fallen asleep during every movie we've ever watched together. I've seen him snore through *Speed* and *Apocalypse Now*. We embrace.

"Nice to see you, kid," he says.

"Happy to see you."

His visits trigger shopping sprees in my wife and daughter, perhaps because they think I'm satiated with a buddy. They can vanish for hours before returning with house stuff, a bathroom rug, a basket for markers, tons of neon girl garb. So I sit with this man, in the kitchen, in the living room, sometimes under the umbrella by the pool. We talk about politics, the eye-rolling news of the day. He also loves food so he gets lost in dreamy monologues about entrées he's loved and lost, a truffle dish he had in the Piedmont region in 1979.

"There's a certain man," he once told me. "His task is to present you with the day's truffles, under glass, the way you'd display a diamond. You pick the one you want, big, small, whatever. He weighs it right there on a tiny scale and starts shaving the thing over your pasta, your eggs, your gelato if you want him to."

I remember him smiling deeply, the smell of it all, the flurries of truffles so crisp in his mind.

Alex enters the room and my father-in-law stands to hug him.

"Hi, Grandpa."

"The man of the house," he says, holding Alex's shoulders. "A growing man."

"Probably four inches since you've seen him, Dad," Jackie says.

"Like a bean sprout. You playing football?"

Alex shakes his head.

"Any sports?"

"No, Grandpa. I don't really . . . think about sports."

My father-in-law nods, pulls Alex into his chest. "I don't either. I'm happy to see your face," he says, and kisses him on the cheek. "How's school?"

"Good."

"Just good?"

"Yeah."

"Well, that's better than bad."

Alex nods and slowly leaves the room with his burrito.

"Is he okay?" my father-in-law asks me.

"He's just a teenager," Jackie says.

"I'm sure you remember Jackie the same way?" I say.

"Not really."

"Would you like a glass of wine, Dad?"

"I would, I would."

I pour some Cabernet and we take our glasses into the den. We all sit and Jackie taps me on the shoulder and points out that my knees are nearly touching my father-in-law's. She loves that I love him but doesn't want me on his lap. I guess I've been hungry for a visit from someone who roots for us unconditionally. The man was an art dealer in New York until Jackie's mom got sick. I find the subject fascinating. So we talk about the history of abstract paintings, the techniques, the strokes, the gestures, the words that do so little to describe one's relationship to any given offering. He gave us the piece over the fireplace and the one over our bed too. The artists' names sound as fluid as the brushstrokes on the pieces and I love and respect him for using his life to learn the language, to place himself in an existence so far from the safety of the drab and conventional grid. Oil and acrylic, canvas and paper. It's so simple, so primal, the grit of the paint created from dirt and dye, sand and soil. The painting above our bed offers a wide and even violent splatter of red that hurls through the middle of a seventy-by-forty inch canvas. Through that, a wider ribbon of black and copper fires up and off the edge of the left corner. Nothing is moving, yet the velocity is loud, raucous, unhinged.

And then, of course, he'll remind you that it's a business too. Cold and final, in which he'd become a salesman who spoke hurriedly to filthy-rich second wives about the importance of the dripping targets above their mantels. "Got anything with horses in it?" he remembers being asked.

As he tells me this story I laugh, picturing him standing there, trying to keep the fish on the line without demolishing the client's store-bought ego. He fires up his electric cigarette and exhales an enormous stream. In the cloud of it all he shakes his head. "Stupid people. Some people are so fuckin' stupid."

I think about taking a hit off the thing. I pass and take a huge sip of wine. My daughter asks if we want to watch a movie tonight. We vote yes and that the movie will be *The Princess Bride*. My wife and I try to think if there are any naked breasts in the film.

I ask my father-in-law if he remembers any boobs in *The Princess Bride*.

"I sure hope so," he says.

"Let's watch *Harry Potter*," my daughter says. "There's no boobs in it."

"No, no, no thank you," my father-in-law says, making a face of great disdain. "I hate that sci-fi crap."

"Oh Grandpa, you don't even know it."

"I saw it."

"When?"

"Maybe I read about it. I like movies about real people. I don't like animation."

"It's not animated, Grandpa."

"But it's like that. I like movies about real life."

He's so funny to me, this man who's not my father or my uncle. He's not my cousin or my friend, really. But he's a major character in my life. When he was younger, with darker hair, more pop to his knees, he'd insist he was born to sell, to go for the jugular without you knowing he was there. My wife says he's always been an old softy, that the toughness is a shield of sorts, protecting his insecurities. She says his childhood was tough, lonely, and poor, overcrowded in closed quarters. But she doesn't know details because he either forgot it all or chooses to keep it private. The past is the past. He'd rather discuss today, tonight, right now.

"I think we should make a roast," he says. "Surround it with fingerling potatoes. You guys have any rosemary?"

There's something heroic about forgetting or ignoring the past and all that swirls in one's memory. Time is better spent getting down to the marrow of your moment, your self, your taste buds. This world has its obvious glooms and joys, its changing seasons, its all-important celebrity updates. The most important lesson I'll take from this man is that the true cruelty of aging is you end up knowing too much. The emperor, and there are dozens of them, hardly ever wears clothes. Pundits gossipers, conspicuous consumers, bill collectors, advertisers, liars, cheaters, and overeaters— it's exhausting. When he's not sitting with me he gets on planes by himself and chills out on beaches a billion miles from all that nags him. The lesson is to find justification in any move, responsible or otherwise, that brings joy to your bloodstream. And hopefully, in the moment you arrive, just as a breeze ruffles your hair from the west, you will feel far enough away.

The Princess Bride it is. Alex says he's seen it.

Derail

Jackie wants to try. With two and a half hours before a business trip to Los Angeles, she pulls me by my belt loop into our room. I'm nude and in bed at 3:23 p.m. I know it's time to tell her. About me, and baby number three. Alex isn't improving. One teacher describes him as asleep with his eyes open. Another, his math teacher, says he's fine with homework but rarely speaks at all. The St. John's wort either did nothing or made it worse. His therapist says half the battle is getting him to open up; lately he just plays with his phone. He thinks we should stop the St. John's wort and consider prescription medicine. I can't think about medicating him without dread, my own grief rising, tempting the notion that I made him this way, even though it's uncertain. Do I want to bring another sad or challenged person into the world? What if it's me, my blood, my genes that have left him so lonely, so alienated in his own skin?

The trying is not happening. She offers some dirty talk to get things going but sneezes during it. She needs a tissue. I hand her one. I wish I were wearing pants.

"This isn't happening, is it?" she says.

"Sorry," I say, and try again. I kiss her. I nuzzle my cheek into hers. The phone rings.

"Don't," she says.

"It could be Alex's school," I say. I pick it up. It's my friend Michael.

"Hey, man, calling about your birthday. Coming up, right?" he says.

"Yeah. Can't talk right now."

"What do you want as a gift? Come up to the city, I'll throw you a bash."

"No, thanks. Gotta call you back." I hang up.

"Michael?" Jackie says.

"Yup."

"Did he ask about your birthday?"

"Yes."

"He called me about it too," she says. "I think he wants us to have a party. What do you want this year?"

"A healthy son."

"We're back!" yells my father-in-law.

My wife flies off the bed and shoots into the bathroom.

"I have Tara," he says. "Anybody home?"

"Yes," Jackie yells. "Down in a second."

I pull some pants on and greet him in the hallway. "Hi there."

"I have the girl only," he says.

"Where's Alex?"

My father-in-law shakes his head. "He told me he had extra work to do. He said you knew about it."

Tara nods.

"Extra work. Alex said he had extra work?"

"That's what he told us."

"Jackie?"

"Yes?"

"Did Alex say anything to you about staying at school for extra work?"

"What?"

"I'm going to the school."

"Why?" she says, opening the bathroom door. "He's fine, Jay. I'll call the school. Don't overreact."

But my mind warns me of trouble, all my nightmares come to life. He never stays after school, not once in my memory.

I park next to the football field and run onto the path and into the woods. I see five, six kids sitting on the logs around the fire. None of them are Alex. I jog back to the school and the door is chained. I find a teacher entrance. I look in every classroom on the floor: 200, 201, 202, 203, 204. In the office I find a woman. She asks me to calm down, to tell her who my son is. I try to talk slower, telling her that his grandfather came to pick him up. Her tone is kind, triggering a sense of loss, doom.

"I have to know where he is," I tell her.

"We'll find him," the woman says, her hand on mine. "We always do."

🖋   🖋   🖋

Third floor. Room 303. Computer lab. Extra work. His teacher is a man in a beret and Wallabees. Alex never discusses school with me, ever. He takes math advice from his mother. I've seen them sit together for an hour. Turns out he has a computer class. I imagine Jackie knows about it. I sit next to him and he pushes play.

"I made this," he says.

A flying dragon descends from a cliff. He aims for a knight in purple armor on a horse. They battle; the dragon breathes fire; the knight jousts and falls to the ground. The dragon incinerates him. A tombstone rises. The end. I ask to see it again. He gladly resets it. I never see him smile but I smell accomplishment on him. I ask to see it again, and one more time.

"It's very good work," I say. "So impressive."

In the parking lot I attempt, without thought, to put my arm around him. He sees it coming, scoots right to dodge the affection. Please don't touch me, he'd say, if he spoke.

In the car I ask him if he'd like to show his movie to the family. He says, "No, thanks," and we leave it at that.

Older

Birthday! My birthday. It feels like I just celebrated forty-five. I'm satiated, don't really need a party. I ask Alex and Tara to join us for dinner but the excursion involves first picking Mommy up at the airport. Tara begs for a sleepover at Ginger's house instead and Alex, well, Alex is not a restaurant person. It's a tapas joint. Jackie looks spent in the car, her eyes unfocused as if she's lost in thought.

"You okay?"

"This job, this job. Let's have a fun birthday."

"Tell me."

"It's the same shit. Let's talk about it tomorrow."

"Now you have to tell me."

"Human resources says layoffs are imminent. Again. Maybe it's just another mind-fuck. I'm in the doghouse according to Piper and Sammy. What can I say?"

"So."

"So break out your resume," she says.

I face her to see how serious she is.

"Really?"

Her shoulders pop up and her smirk is broken but sweet. "Trouble in paradise."

I order the largest pitcher of sangria they have and consider life with no income. What do you do? That will be the question. What is it that you are doing? You mean right now? Oh, you mean my job. I see. Lately, um, I got a new one. I sit on a barstool in the nude for a pencil drawing class at the New School. In other words, I'm paid to let people stare at and draw my genitals. I am also an oil fireman. So, no water used. They do not mix. I also manufacture the circular plastic discs one finds lodged in bottle caps. I pick the mud out of hooved animals at the zoo. I vacuum cockpits. I'm a fifth-string bull pen catcher. I'm a volunteer collaborator. Regional vice manager of Birds Eye frozen foods: edamame division. I work at a Fotomat. I work in the screw section at Ace. I'm a copywriter. The last packaging I did was for a motorcycle game for the PC. *Ready to Soar Zero to Sixty in a TT Bike Blink?* That's right, I wrote that.

"SURPRISE!!!!!"

Surreal, as a dream. My eyes blown wide with the faces of my friends, all walking inside the restaurant in a line. It's all of them. Nicky and Michael, their wives, even Ray and Lizzie. A part of me wishes it wasn't real. A surprise party. Yeah. My date night birthday with my wife is over. Michael's the first to embrace me. He wants me to know it was his idea, to fly everyone down. I'm surrounded by loving looks and extra-hard hugs, my face pressed into the stubble of sweet men. The waiter moves us to a bigger table and brings five pitchers out. I fill everyone's glass to the rim.

"You flew here, for me, my God, Michael. You paid, that's nuts."

"All for you, my friend."

"That's so nice, man. Really great."

Ten sips in and I'm partying with my high school friends and my wife is the most gorgeous of all the organisms to sprout from the earth. Too bad Gigi insisted on seating the men as far from their spouses as the table allows.

"A toast," Michael says, his sangria in the air. "To an amazing friend, a birthday wish for you. May your life remain healthy and your children flourish! Happy birthday, Jay!"

Within minutes, Michael, Nick, and Ray are ready to sing the song that brought us together on the Little League field.

Hate to talk about your mother but you talked about mine.
She's got meatball tits and a rubber behind.
Hanging out the window with her dick in her hand
Yelling, "Hey motherfucker, I'm Superman."

The group remembers it well. Joanna admits to always hating the song. I believe we sang it too loud.

Michael stands again. "Another toast. To our hosts."

Everyone touches glasses and my wife and I blow kisses to each other.

Joanna stands next. "Happy birthday, Jay! To love, children, and sangria!"

"Yeah!"

Nicholas stands. "Happy birthday to my man Jay. To love, sangria, and moments just like now, with all of you . . . without the kids. I love adult swim."

"Cheers!"

My wife stands and I smile, waiting to hear her version of the pattern.

"I love you, Jay."

Awwww!

"Happy, happy birthday, my love. To our kids, to this sangria. And to the fact that we're trying to have a *baby!*"

Oh no. The women all stand. They engulf her. Nick bumps his head against Jackie's shoulder. "Don't you get it?" he says. "You're done. Your kids have lives, agendas, places to be. You're free. Why would you do that to yourself?"

My wife ignores him; she's beaming. "We just feel like someone's missing from our table."

Awwww!

I nod. And I keep nodding. "That's how we feel," I say. "That's how we both feel."

I look at my wife. She's grinning her brains out. I ask myself if it feels like someone is indeed missing from our table. I see my son. I see my little girl.

"To hotel sex!" yells Gigi, and our glasses touch again.

Ray, seated next to my wife, has a sangria mustache. I know he's a whisky guy so this stuff probably tastes like Hawaiian punch to him. I picture the ambulance we'll need to get him out of here. Lizzie, who happened to be seated next to me, has disappeared. She'd been sitting here, silently, playing with an Ace bandage on her wrist. I'd say it's been a half hour. I try to make eye contact with Ray but he's sloshed.

"Raymond," I say.

He faces Michael. Michael points at me.

"Lizzie's been gone awhile. Go take a look."

He looks around for her with an extended neck and then stands to find her. I move my seat closer to my wife and find the girls are getting catty. Joanna and Gigi are having no trouble expressing their scorn for Lizzie. As happens in most drunken gatherings of American sorority alumnae, the moment is devoted to unhinging one member from the pack. Lizzie isn't here, she's wearing lesser clothing, and her hair is done provincially. She is doomed in this group. Suddenly my liberal, middle-aged mom friends have become superior enough to slur in giggling whispers, "Crack is wack, Lizzie."

"If she's doing drugs in the bathroom I'd like to try some," says Joanna. "I feel left out."

Everyone laughs, even my wife.

"Meth," says Gigi, sipping her drink. "Or ketamine."

"OxyContin," says Nick. "You can tell from her skin."

"I just hope she brought enough for all of us," says Michael.

We see Ray with Lizzie, but of course they're fighting, dramatically, in the nice restaurant. It's not the prom, for Christ's sake; we're too old for this. Lizzie cocks her fist and punches him hard in the shoulder. He rubs it as they walk back to us, his bottom lip between his teeth.

"There you are," I say, pretending I saw nothing. Lizzie sits and unravels her Ace bandage. The waitress delivers more plates, things I had no idea were ordered. None of us eats much but the pitchers of sangria keep coming. I can hear only two of the conversations at the table. Lizzie and I are the only people not engaged in one. Once she gets the bandage back on, she clamps it and grabs her drink.

"How's Katrina's school year been, Lizzie?"

She wasn't expecting the Inquisition.

"What?"

"I was wondering about Katrina's school year. I'm sure she's writing a lot, she likes it so much."

"I don't know. She seems to like it." She nods, glances at the other ladies and gulps her drink. "She might make honor roll."

"Terrific. Terrific, Liz. That's big. That's good news. I really love it when she opens that notebook."

She perks up as I do, the infectiousness of joy.

"Ray doesn't even know," she says. "Hey, Ray!"

Ray is kneeling between Michael and Joanna. He plays the little boy with his parents, promising it's all going to get better soon, mentioning the jobs on the horizon, the impressive-sounding college classes. He says "Business 101" and "Economics for the Small Business Venture," and even though he's not employed today he predicts he will be soon. Ray bends his fingers back as he counts his prospects. Mommy Joanna has her hand on his shoulder; she messes his hair. How the hell did I get stuck at this end with Lizzie? Because no one, including Ray, the schmuck she lives with, wants to sit next to her. I look at Lizzie, done trying to reach Ray. Her eyes lower and lock on her phone.

"Lizzie?" I say.

"Yeah?"

"Can you pass me the sangria?"

She lifts the pitcher and pours us both a refill. I get a smile from her. I'm speaking her language.

"I can drink this stuff all night," she says. Lizzie and I clank our glasses and take large sips. She laughs and points at my face. "Your teeth are purple."

"Yours too," I say, and she covers her mouth with her hand. When I face Ray he sees me having fun with Lizzie. I decide it's the best gift I can give him. I pour us another glass and try to conjure a memory that Lizzie will also recall. I remember horrific nights in which she and Ray would physically fight and one of the rest of us would be peeling them off each other in some parking lot. Their screaming matches and eye-gouging on humid, tedious summer nights became our staple memories on hungover mornings. Even at the prom, Ray tore some crucial part off her dress, nine seconds after we picked her up. They got sloshed and never remembered.

"Remember the prom?" I ask her. It's all I got.

Her face has relaxed. I can see her personality. "I remember gettin' wasted."

I nod. "Yeah. We did that a lot."

She takes a huge gulp and glances down the table at Ray. "He's such a jerk," she says. Apparently the best way to bond with Lizzie is to bash Ray.

"Hey Ray!" she barks again.

I put my hand on hers. "Let him talk. He loves to talk. People who talk as much as Ray should have a talk show, don't ya think?"

"Hey, asshole!" she screams, my hand still on hers.

Gigi and Joanna look over at Lizzie.

"You too important to answer me?"

Ray stands from his crouch. "Shut the hell up, Liz. I'm talking to people with brains."

"Oh, I'm sure you're stimulating all of them with your hopes and dreams."

Ray walks back to our end and sits with a grinding jaw. "You can't let me talk to my friends? Are you really that fuckin' insecure?"

Lizzie hides behind her glass, as all the wives gawk at her.

I think about a toast to change the subject.

"Let's toast!"

"Can't you just let me have a life that doesn't involve you, Liz? Is that so hard for you? To leave me the hell alone!"

The waitress comes over.

"Hi," I say, hoping she can help us. But she can't.

Lizzie is standing, gathering her purse.

"Sit down, Liz," Ray says.

"No!"

"Sit the hell down."

"No! *You!*"

"I have to say this," Joanna says, standing. "I'm really feeling that the two of you are trying to make this night about you, when in fact it's about Jay. Right? Isn't tonight about a birthday party and being with friends?"

Lizzie is staring at Joanna with murderous eyes. She's been in her company since their plane left Newark at noon. I envision a strangulation. My wife walks over to Lizzie and asks to speak to her in private. Lizzie responds by lifting the remaining pitcher of sangria and hurling it at Ray. Nicky and Gigi get the most wet. Ray's hair gets hit but not his body.

The management asks us to leave. Joanna uses her most diplomatic tone, trying to appease the manager, even showing him some form of ID.

"Please leave," the man says.

Joanna loses. We all pour out into the parking lot. None of this will be funny for years.

The Boot

Jackie drives the minivan Michael rented and we leave our car in the parking lot. The silence adds to the drama, the harried crime of it all. What a joke, the circus we are, so moronic, a bunch of hotheaded middle-aged drinkers. I've probably had four birthdays where Lizzie threw something on Ray and ruined the night. It's just par.

"Thanks for driving, Jackie," I say.

"Happy birthday," she says solemnly.

"Sorry that happened."

"I didn't know you were designated," Michael says from the back.

"Benefit of baby making," my wife says.

"Sangria goes down quick," I say.

"Especially for some people," says Gigi.

"Tssa," comes out of my wife's mouth.

"What kind of noise was that?" I ask.

"Tssa," she says again. "Quiet time."

I stare at her. Rude. Quieting me. On my birthday. I did nothing. I drank, ate, and got booted.

"I have to say something," Gigi says.

Please don't.

"It's really too bad you have to get so fucking drunk, Lizzie. So drunk that you felt it was appropriate to throw a full pitcher of sangria, that you didn't even pay for, all over me."

"Who cares about *you?*" Lizzie snaps.

"I do! You're paying for my dry cleaning and my phone, you *bitch.*"

Lizzie doesn't do well inebriated. Can you tell? She's up, out of her seat, diving with her nails aimed at the spot the word *bitch* came from. I reach over the front seat to grab Lizzie's kneecaps, trying to pull her back. But she's on Gigi. My wife keeps driving through the mayhem and then pulls over. The car fishtails, the tires screech on the pavement. We all jolt forward. Screams, tears, threats of lawsuits, torn clothing, and cheek-rattling fury is a description of the next four minutes. Ray ends the attack on Gigi by using Lizzie's ponytail as a rope to get her off. "Fuckin' *stop*, Liz!"

The drive home from that spot changes us as a clique. It's irreparable for Lizzie and Ray, the end of their connection to the others. My forehead is definitely scratched. I lost the three middle buttons on this shirt I liked. My wife is beyond upset. Blaming me will be the most productive for her. I long for the clean slate of the morning. Back in the driveway everyone scatters, ready to get away from each other, see if they're injured. My wife checks on Alex and is gone, to the bedroom, alone. I check my face. I think I got caught by Joanna's wedding ring. I turn the TV on in the den and hear Ray in the hallway. He's dialing, has his suitcase at his feet.

"Ray?"

"I'm done, man. It's over. I'm not gonna let my daughter live with that lunatic. No more, no way."

"We'll go to sleep, like we always do. We'll figure it out together in the morning."

"No. It's over. It's over this time. I'm out of here."

"You have to calm down, gather your thoughts. Assess it all in the morning."

"I'm done assessing."

"Go to bed. You just got here. You flew for my birthday." I reach for his arm.

"Get off, man. Happy birthday, you're my best friend. Now get off."

"If you fight me," I whisper, trying to be funny, "it's going to make a ton of noise."

"It doesn't matter," he says, and lifts me off the ground. The man is either furious or on steroids but he places me out of his way like an empty box.

"Ray?"

"Good-bye, Jay."

"You're leaving Lizzie here?" I try to say quietly. "Is she your parting gift?"

"Keep her! Tell her I'm going to get Katrina. We're *done!*"

"You tell her. She's upstairs. Go talk to her."

Michael walks out of his room and joins me. He's wearing pajama bottoms and no shirt and sips a Gatorade. "This moron. What's he doing now?"

"What does it look like?"

"Looks like he's leaving," he says. "Without Queen Happiness?"

I run upstairs to get Lizzie and she's facedown on the bed. I shake her.

"Lizzie, Ray is leaving. You have to get up."

She's out. I hear a car out front. Through the window I see Ray get in the cab.

"Lizzie. He says he's going to get Katrina. *Liz!*"

Release Me

Choppy sleep. Sugary alcohol, and then adrenaline on top. At 6:00 a.m. I'm up and find Gigi in the kitchen. She's over the sink in a tank top, trying to see an abrasion under her armpit. I startle her and she faces me horrified.

"Sorry," I say.

"Jesus."

"Didn't mean to scare you."

"I thought you were Liz."

"Sorry. You okay?"

"Yeah. Love being scratched and punched by white trash." She shuts the water off. "I don't care if she doesn't have two nickels to rub together, there's consequences for attacking people."

There's another scratch on her cheek that runs down to her chin. We hear someone coming down the back stairs. It's my father-in-law, in a robe and bare feet. "What are you doing up?" he says.

It takes him a minute to recognize Gigi. And even in the embrace she's helping him recall. "I'm one of Jackie's best friends."

"Of course," he says warmly. "Of course. Gigi."

"Nice to see you again," she says.

"How was the surprise?" he asks me.

"I was very surprised. I did not see that coming."

"Jay!" my wife yells in a whisper. She's on the staircase, her robe closed with clutched arms. "Try to wake her. It's time for her to leave. I want to have a nice day."

I find Lizzie with her face mashed into the mattress, her mouth blocked to breathe. I sit next to her and rub her back. "Lizzie? Can we talk?" Nothing. I doubt she realizes or cares she's been officially exiled from the group, removed from the playbill, traded to another league. I shake her again and she's awake. Her eyes look punched, saliva on her chin. I smell fruity-stale fermented air.

"Let's talk," I say. "Okay?"

It takes a minute but she sits up, rubs her face, and yawns before asking, "Where's Ray at?"

"He left last night."

Her eyes leap to mine. "What?" She stands, her gaze pinned on me. "*What?*"

"I did everything I could. He was drunk and you know how he can be."

"I'm calling the police."

"He's gone, Lizzie. Probably landed in Newark."

"He's going to take her from me," she says, and removes her T-shirt over her head, exposing her breasts. "I need a ride to the airport." She looks around the room, lost, confused. "Where are my shoes?"

I point at her Crocs. "I'll be in the car."

Lizzie's dialing Ray again and I'm driving over eighty just to end this part of my day.

"He won't pick it up. That scumbag won't pick up."

There's some life to her now, so much purpose. Perhaps this is Lizzie's calling. Someone who hunts down those who've wronged her. It's probably how they communicate best, by playing monkey in the middle with the little girl they spawned. Heartache can be vicious but to truly tap into the bite is a gift. I hate them both.

"Cocksucker won't pick up."

I cannot live with this particular friend in my life anymore. Upon dropping Lizzie at the airport curb I will graduate from Ray and his girlfriend. Katrina, poor soul, a sweetie, a pawn in her parents' callous existence. I swear I'd steal her from them and raise her as my own if they'd only drop off the earth. But that's no remedy. Lizzie slams her phone down on her pillow and stares out the window.

"Can I say something . . . Lizzie?"

She faces me.

"There's a little girl in the middle of this."

"What do you mean?"

"I mean Katrina."

"You don't think I know that?"

"She's not like a . . . piece in a board game."

"What?"

"You're using her as currency."

"*He* treats her like that."

"Everything she sees she absorbs," I say. "As an adult she'll be a zillion little pieces of her experiences, right? She's being shaped now, as a person, by you and Ray and everything you offer her."

She grinds her teeth, mistaking my words as inspiration for rage.

"If he takes my daughter from me I will kill him. Let *him* feel what it's like to have your kid taken from you. Just wait, just wait." Her smile is maniacal but the rainbow pillowcase on her lap steals her thunder. I'd let her out here if I could. On the highway. When my phone vibrates in my pocket I decide to ignore it. Just drive and end this. It rings again so I reach for it. It's my brother Cam.

"You sound like you're in a wind tunnel," he says before hello.

"I'm driving."

"Good. I've got your full attention."

Lizzie's dialing Ray again. I pull off the highway for the Tampa airport.

"This isn't easy for me," Cam says. "But it's important I share it with you, as I'm told my own reporting of the issue will be cathartic."

"What? You need to speak louder."

"I'm in love with someone else," is all I hear. "And I'm leaving Kate."

I stay silent, hearing only the click of Lizzie dialing and the whir of the road. I can see Kimmy's face in my thoughts, my mother, my sister-in-law.

"I've fallen in love. I can't believe it when I say it. But I've fallen in love with the most incredible woman."

"I'm flying United," Lizzie says and unfolds her boarding pass.

"I'm in love for the first time, Jay. Kate is not an easy person to love. In fact, I am *repulsed* by her and her phony pride in herself."

"Did you hear me?" Lizzie asks.

"I hate sleeping next to her. I hate waking up next to her; but mostly—and I wanted you, my brother, to hear this from me—I hate the way she makes me feel about myself. I hate being the person who hates her. I hate hating her. I hate myself for marrying her. The only thing I got in the deal was Kimmy."

I pull up to the departing flights curb and Lizzie gets out without saying good-bye.

"Are you still there?" my brother says.

"Yes."

Lizzie has her bag. She knocks on the window and I open it.

"Thanks," she says.

I nod, and wave. She shuffles away, her plastic shoes clomping with each step.

"Say something," Cam says. "It isn't helpful if you say nothing."

"I need to call you back," I say, now alone in my car.

"I was hoping for a reaction," he says. "Any reaction to what I just told you. I'm in love, man, for the first time, Jay."

"I'll call you back," I say, and hang up.

Just outside the airport, there's a thin lane of pavement that extends along the runway. If you park there and wait for the next takeoff you can witness the gargantuan belly of the aircraft as it ascends. The climb upward requires jets, so the sound is a rage of engine thrust and hydraulic muscle. The human ear can barely take it. I hold my breath with my stomach clenched as a sadness engulfs me, and tears ring too trite. My brother doesn't know yesterday was my birthday. But he called me anyway. A plane gains altitude and I lower the window to hear the rapture. I'm comforted by how small I am inside the roar. The machine rockets higher, and soon banks left.

Help

I dial my mother and think of the words I might use. Cam is leaving. Cam is cheating. Cam is done with his marriage. I get her
voice mail.

"Just confirming Thanksgiving," I say. "We'll be there on
Thursday morning. Kids are good. Bye for now."

In the kitchen, Joanna, Nick, Jackie, and Gigi are eating with
my father-in-law. He lowers his eyeglasses from his forehead to see
me. "Heard about last night," he says. "So happy I missed it."

"Yeah. I don't blame you."

"Look at all of you," he says. "Hangovers kill men my age. You
all look green."

"Thanks, Dad."

"You made the right choice," says Nick.

"I remember Jackie's thirty fifth," my father-in-law says. "Remember? The theme drink was mojitos?"

Jackie and Joanna recall the night viscerally. It triggers nausea.

"Let's talk about something else," my wife says.

Alex walks in the kitchen, wishing he'd checked the room before entering. His mouth opens to speak then closes, his arms at his side. So many people, so many questions. He blinks as they fire. "*Alex!*" The guests stand, hug him, wait their turn to greet him. He eyes me as Gigi takes his thin frame in her grip. "How are you?"

"Good."

Playing sports? Got a girlfriend? Do you miss San Francisco? How you liking Florida?

"No. No. No. Good."

Jackie stands to kiss him, sneaking it in as if she's an aunt or something. She holds him and he doesn't squirm so I try next but he sees me coming. "No," he says, and the moms laugh. Teenagers. Alex tries to smile and turns to leave the room. He finds Michael in the doorway. "Alex!"

"Hi."

"How are you?"

"Good."

"Great, so good to see you, man. You've grown, wow, look at you."

"He's like a bean sprout," my father-in-law says.

"He's so handsome," Joanna says.

They know he struggles. Friends ask about kids, good friends hear the truth. He's not interested in making friends. Here, back in California, no thanks. He slinks out of the room, forgoing whatever he came in for. My father-in-law waves me over to him. People are chatting so I kneel to hear him. "Last night he left the house. For about an hour. What's he doing out there?" he asks.

"He left for an hour?"

"About that. I figured he was nearby, maybe seeing a friend. When he came back he went right to his room."

"Will you go ask him?" I say.

"Now?"

"Yes. Just say, 'Where did you go last night?' Would you?"

My father-in-law nods like Robert De Niro. He's up and out, heading for Alex.

My mind races. I see him in the yard alone. If it's just reclusiveness, then I need to hear it's healthy. The group laughs in the kitchen.

"So they're gone," says Gigi. "The Munsters have left."

Michael snorts. "The Munsters. Perfect."

"I feel badly about it all," my wife says. "But I feel for Katrina the most."

The idea of those people raising Katrina. A person so ready to learn and go. Her influences are rooted in them. Ray and Lizzie—Parents of the Year. My father-in-law is back too quick. He stands in the doorway of the dining room.

"He says he likes to sit in the backyard."

"Okay."

"He says it helps him remember."

"Remember what?"

"I don't know."

"You didn't ask?"

"I didn't want to intrude."

"Please go back."

He sighs and I spin him, force him to do an about-face. I decide to wait where I'm standing. He trudges back up the stairs. My wife joins me. I tell her what I know.

"He's up there with him now?"

Her cell phone rings. Tara's ready to be picked up from Ginger's house.

"Anyone want to take a ride to the beach?" I say.

Michael raises his hand.

"Let's get Tara."

In the car, Michael rests his bare feet on the dashboard. He's telling me about his new job but I can only listen in spurts. I think of Alex, walking alone in the night. He finds a stump or a patch of grass to sit on. He looks up at the sky, the moon, and the beams of white that splay from the edges.

"Private practice has its drawbacks," says Michael. "But hospital life is rough."

If Alex had diabetes we'd medicate him. I long for the most banal of scenarios and weaken at the idea of the medicine backfiring and yanking the wires from his young brain. They say it can take months to get the right medication and dosage. If it were his knee I'd hold it, massage it, pray my DNA mattered in the warmth of skin on skin. But he's distant and turned off, needs time to age, maybe, before allowing me in, if ever. Does he need me at all, subtly, profoundly? I cannot get my hands around his brain.

Michael's story has ended. I nod and feel badly I wasn't present.

"Everything okay with Alex?" he asks.

I face him. "I think he's better, I do."

"He's probably got girls on the mind, right?"

I shake it off and smile. "You would've laughed, man. When we first arrived he went through a 'what's a three-some?' stage. 'Is boning the same as banging?'"

"Really?" he says and laughs.

"Yeah, we laugh a lot. He's doing fine, just fine."

"Good, good to hear. I have patients his age. The growing pains. They hate everyone, even themselves sometimes. The pubescent brain can be cruel. Not easy. Can be lonely."

I nod.

"You notice the way he carries his shoulders? Like he aches with the weight of them? His bone growth is literally staggering."

"And puberty," I say.

"Right, right," he says. "And maybe some depression."

Michael's a pediatrician, so I let the word float out there. Swallow my innate need to defend. I'd give a limb to see my boy wake with a smile and head off with joy in his step. I need him to live and breathe on even terrain. I pull off the highway toward the beach and decide to change the subject.

"Michael?"

"Yeah?"

"You ever think of getting a vasectomy?"

"What? No. I thought Jackie said you're trying."

I pull into Ginger's driveway and put the car in park. "It's not going to happen."

"No, huh?"

"I'm not trying anymore."

"Does Jackie know this?"

"No."

"Okay."

"Do you know any urologists?" I ask.

He nods but his face is forlorn. "I know a dozen."

"Will you email the info?"

"You sure? Hard to reverse."

Teri walks out of the front door with Tara on her arm. Ginger blows bubbles behind them. I introduce Michael to Teri and she remembers him from that day at the Mahanley River.

"I remember you too," he says, and looks her up and down, this Florida Barbie with a brain. Today she wears jean shorts, the mirrored glasses, and an AC/DC T-shirt. Her legs have been oiled professionally. A toned glaze, airbrushed by the Lord himself.

"I want to show you something," she says to us and guides us through her front hallway, out to her deck. Large abstract paintings line her walls and I see a record collection, real vinyl, and a tall black case for the stereo. An ocean view, a gazebo, a pool, and a redwood porch that hovers out over a white sand beach. She's rich. Teri points to the right, the corner of the raised structure.

"That's where I'd write if I were a writer," she says. We walk to the spot and she asks me to try it, to sit in the wicker chair provided. "Tara says you're writing a book."

"Really," says Michael. "Is it based on the stuff you read me?"

"I'm just in the notes stage right now. It's a ridiculous spot, I'd write here every day if I could."

"Feel free. Just put me in the acknowledgements."

Michael looks at me, a smirk. I ignore him.

"Deal," I say and crane my neck to the water. The blue of the sky finds the lightest of grays and then darkens. The rain arrives in drizzles and builds as if controlled by a volume knob. The water that falls is warm.

"Thanks so much for the sleepover, Teri," I say, walking through the house. "We'll do it at our place next time. Sound good?"

"Tara is always welcome. Hey, Jay, you guys buy tickets for the sock hop yet?"

"No, a sock hop? Really?"

"You didn't get the flyer?"

"Maybe we did. I'll check."

"You have to come. It's for the children's hospital."

"Oh, okay, I will."

"We also need some help with setup," she says. "Let me know if you can lend a hand. Just call me."

Not long after we pull out of Teri's driveway, a storm hits, for real; my windshield wipers are already out of breath. I'm driving fifteen miles per hour on Interstate 275. The puddles form quick and tug at my tires in spots. When we arrive at my house it's impossible to get inside without being drenched. We run, we laugh, Tara enters the kitchen looking as if she's been dumped in a pool. I find my father-in-law in the den, the *New York Times* hiding all of him.

"Looks like we have a storm," I say.

"My flight could be cancelled tomorrow," he says. "Might have to fly Wednesday."

"Did you talk to Alex again?" I ask.

He lowers the paper and dips his glasses to see me. "He says he sits at the picnic table because he can think better when he's outside. He seems okay. He might just be kind of a loner."

"Don't say that."

"A thinker?"

"Better."

"He is what he is."

"He's fourteen."

"That's probably the best way to look at it," he says.

"He won't talk to me."

"You're his father."

"But he'll talk to you."

He nods.

"I need you."

"I'm here."

"Can you stay another week?"

His head tilts as he ponders it. "For my grandson?" he says, and smiles.

"Thank you."

The newspaper lifts and my father-in-law disappears. I walk to the window to see the rain and it's a true deluge, as if each drop weighs a pound. The water is already pooling up the curb, searching for the walkway to my front door.

"One more thing," my father-in-law says.

I face the newspaper.

"He doesn't love the shrink."

A Stranger Arrives

The area around the patient's scrotum will be shaved and cleaned with an antiseptic solution to reduce the chance of infection. A small incision is made into the scrotum. Each of the vasa deferentia (one from each testicle) is tied in two places with nonabsorbable (permanent) sutures and the tube is severed between the ties. The ends may be cauterized (burned or seared) to decrease the chance that they will leak or grow back together.

This is the email I get from Michael while he's still at my house. I read it as my wife learns I've asked her father to stay longer. She was ready for privacy, she says, the type you don't get in the presence of your parents.

"Alex talks to him," I repeat.

"Alex talks to me."

"He does?"

"When we do homework."

"What does he say?"

"Some of it is private."

"Are you kidding me? Private between who?"

"He's told me not to tell you certain things."

I cannot believe this. He won't say a word to me and he's asking his mother to do the same.

"I think you're lonely," she says. "And that's why you want my dad to stay."

She's trying to start a fight. I'll take the high road.

"I disagree."

"Your friends are leaving. You don't have anyone outside the family here."

"Alex told your dad he doesn't like Dr. Zinnman. Did you know that?"

"That's not even true."

"Yes," I say.

"I'll ask him about it."

"We wouldn't have known. If not for your dad."

"My dad has a life he needs to get back to, Jay. I'll talk to Alex."

"We'd be sending him to that office forever and he doesn't even like the guy. I knew we should've gone with the lady."

"My dad probably misunderstood. But if he's unhappy we'll switch."

"Switch?"

"Try another doctor. It's a process. The person, the meds, we're chasing it down."

She steps to me and tries to unfold my arms. I won't let her. She tells me that as soon as the rain stops, her father is leaving for the airport with our friends. She then reminds me that I made a date with a man from the school. I booked it the night we attended teacher conferences. Oh, right. Beers with a painter named Paul. He's the only father I know at the kids' school with a ponytail. I tend to get along with long-haired men. We were destined to find each other, the only two dads in the building who inhaled. I tell my wife I'd be glad to go out with Paul the hippie but that I am not lonely for men. She asks if I'm lonely for women. Only you. *BOOM!* The conversation ends with an explosion of thunder. It sounds like a locomotive was catapulted into my backyard and when I get there I'm expecting to see the charred detritus of my lounge chairs. All seems okay but the electricity is out. The rain is relentless and my street is an overflowing lake. All five guests are stuck here because the minivan they rented is way too low in this water. It could flood, stall out. There are kayaks and small rafts floating down the road and my lawn is a riverbed, seemingly drowning.

Michael, Nick, and I sit on my porch. The water is already on my front walkway, taunting us as it inches higher. The topic of discussion is whether we move the furniture upstairs. The wood floors would be ruined, lost. I thank God my friends are here and can still lift sofas. The electricity pops back on and I hear applause. We hover around the TV and the weatherman says, "Get those sandbags out."

I see Alex in the kitchen, staring out at the density of the downpour. His eyes meet mine, seeking assurance, I like to think. I nod and smile at him, proving I don't need words either. He walks away. Joanna is panicky, texting with the vigor of the trapped. *What about my children? How the hell do I get out of Florida? Jay and his stupid birthday. So much fun!!* Another *BOOM* of thunder has all my picture frames bouncing. I hear a real scream. Joanna's hand is on her heart.

And then it stops. Light pours in through all the windows. The sun is back. And within a half hour, Joanna and Gigi are *schvitzing* again, talking humidity. The lake recedes. The minivan is loaded, my father-in-law included. The hugs last a while.

I sleep for three hours and wake up to a kiss from my wife. She is dressed for work, a slick black suit.

"Where ya headed?"

"New York. One night. It's been on the calendar."

I get another kiss on the lips but I might be dreaming. I wake up an hour later. The ponytailed painter dad is calling me. He wants to know where we should meet for drinks. I suggest a place downtown called Tryst. As I shower and shave and find my expensive jeans, I feel stupid primping for a man. Sort of pathetic. A blind date. Might be more fun with a woman, right?

The doorbell rings and Tara runs for it.

"Ask who it is," I say, but through the frosted glass I see him. A man about my height with his arms at his sides. It's my brother. My brother Cam is on my porch. His smile is tight, close-mouthed, his hair unslicked. He's wearing shorts and a long-sleeved T-shirt. A suitcase in his grip.

"Surprise," he says, his eyes jumping from me to the kids to the walls of the front hall.

"No way," I say.

He steps in and offers his hand to my daughter. "Hi, remember me? I'm your uncle Cam."

"I know who you are," she says.

Alex walks out of his room, pokes his head over the railing.

"It's your uncle," I say. "Come down for a second."

Alex descends the staircase and offers his hand to Cam.

"What are you feeding this guy?" Cam says. "Wow, look at him."

Alex nods. They clasp hands, bump torsos.

"And where's the lady of the house?"

"You're looking at her," says my daughter.

"Ha, I love this kid. Funny, very funny."

"She's in New York for the night," I say. "Listen, man, it's a crazy surprise to see you. But I was just on my way out."

"Not trying to get in your way. I'm just here for two or three nights."

We stare at each other for a moment. Flies down without a call, invites himself for days?

"Okay."

He steps closer and drops his suitcase. "I know it's sudden. I had to get out of there."

"You mean New York?"

"I mean my house."

I look at my daughter.

"How's Kimmy?" I ask.

He rubs the stubble on his chin before reaching in his pockets with both hands. He comes out with a piece of paper. "Look at this wording from Kate's lawyer."

Circled in yellow neon are the words *visitation denied*. He smiles but looks wounded. "She's taking my kid from me."

"Daddy?" says my daughter.

"Yes?" I say, folding the paper.

"Are you staying home now?"

"No, no," I say, checking my watch. "I have to go meet this guy."

Cam takes the letter from my hand and returns it to his pocket. "Mind if I come along?"

My brother asking me if he can join me to do anything? I nod as I take it all in. "You want to come?"

"Sure. Let me see St. Petersburg."

I ask Alex if he'll carry Cam's bag to the guest room. His shoulders lift and drop and he does it. Cam tips him a twenty-dollar bill and Alex stares at it in his palm.

"Thank you," he mumbles.

I announce what my daughter's bedtime will be and she fights it. I say yes to R-rated movies but ask her to text me the titles. I walk out to the driveway and hear my brother close the door behind us. Just the two of us, heading out on the town. In the car my brother hardly speaks. He's too busy nibbling on the side of his thumb. I ask him what he's doing and he stops. He lowers the window and leans his head out.

"Just thinking," he says. "The second I left I began to feel so free. Because I am." "It's as if I'd been waiting until now for my life to start."

I nod, thinking of Kimmy. The tears he'll ignore, that soak into her pillowcase.

"We close?" he says.

I point, and park the car.

Inside Tryst I see the painter near the pool table. I introduce him to Cam. My brother shakes the guy's hand without eye contact and lifts a pool cue.

"I got winners," he says to the couple playing.

"You need to get quarters at the bar," the man says.

Cam asks if we want drinks.

"Bud," says the painter. "Thanks."

"Sounds good," I say.

Alone with the man, I ask what kind of work he does. He leans in and says, "Oil." He is really pensive, almost too deep to speak. I have to work at it. After Cam gets beers and quarters, he begins to play eight ball. I finish mine fast and order some tequila. Within three sips I can ask old Paul if he likes baseball. He does. Awesome. I tell him I used to play. Even past high school. He says he was an awkward athlete, that his memories of all sports come down to elementary school and the way his lack of dexterity was mocked by his classmates. He recalls this with pained eyes. The silence persists. I watch my brother, the return of his personality. He tells the woman he's playing she needs to keep at least one foot on the floor. I put four bucks in the jukebox: Dire Straits, Rolling Stones, Zeppelin. We drink our cocktails. I do have similar hair to this guy. I guess I need him. Because his mind functions similarly, fires the way mine does. He looks miserable. Inches from cutting his own ear off. But we're like-minded, so perfect. An hombre in the Deep South. We artists need solitude to be productive and productivity to earn our solitude. But we are human. It's lonely to think I need this man to like me.

A school dad we both know named Herb approaches our table. He's huge, stomach out to here and hammered on Stolichnaya. He drinks with us for a while and tells eight or so racist knock-knock jokes. He then wipes an amazing amount of sweat off his forehead and says, "My wife's cheating on me."

Is anyone still married but me?

The artist and I are both silenced, saddened, the alcohol beginning to work against us.

"She's a better parent than me." Herb takes a long sip of his vodka. He looks at me and grins before slamming his glass down. "Maybe I'll just kill her."

"I need another beer," says the painter. He leaves to get another round.

Cam is finished after two games. He got beat by the lady he was scolding, which is funny. Even better, she has pink hair and combat boots. I have to smile; winning for him is like oxygen. He walks over to us, shaking his head.

"What happened?" I ask.

"That freaky chick just cleared the table." He looks back at her. I can see Kimmy's eyes in my brother's, the same light green.

"I want a rematch," he says, and heads to the bar for more quarters.

I'm left with sloshed Herb. He begins a knock-knock joke and I decide ahead of time not to say "Who's there?" It works. A girl near the bar screams, "Stop!" as she's tickled by her muscular boyfriend. The ape spins her and places her on the ground.

Cam is back, his gait filled with purpose. He leans over the pool table to break, one eye closed. In his head the whole room is watching the perfect man shoot the perfect ball. He makes his shot and bows to no applause. His smile is infectious, leaves him looking innocent, adorable if you don't know him. He leans close to a woman who wants to talk to him. They both laugh with their heads back. She's in her forties, wears a Buccaneers tank top and knee-high boots. She is liking him, smiling, slapping his shoulder, and now removing her phone from her purse. She hands it to him and he dips his head to dial. How fast was that? A half hour? Why isn't his mistress on his mind? He is *not* bringing this lady back to my house. She's loving his shtick, eating up every word. She lifts his left hand to see if there's a ring. No ring. In minutes she backs her butt into his, swaying to the music. He catches my eye and wants me to see his new girlfriend. Not bad, right? his eyes ask me. Not bad at all. And they approach.

"Hey," I say.

"This is Anna," he says.

"Hi."

"This is my brother."

"I know you," she says. "Your kids go to my kid's school."

I get a better look at her. It's true. She's the mother of my daughter's classmate. "I do know you. We met at orientation."

The woman is a member of a gaggle of similar-looking women in the area. The dress code is young with lots of baby-doll dresses, augmented breasts, and finger bling. They are blond, play tennis and golf at the club, and are in second marriages with rich but shrinking old men. Anna, however, is divorced.

"Your daughter is so beautiful," she says.

"So is yours." Not sure which kid she is.

Her hand grips the back of my arm. "That's so sweet."

I think her eyes have light orange contact lenses in them. Orange? She looks like a leopard. Yes, it's sexy; yes, she's sexy. My brother drapes his arms over her as if they've been married for years.

"Our turn," he says and hands her a pool stick. "You want me to break?"

She cups his chin in her palm and leans in to kiss his cheek. "You bet I do."

My brother's adjustment to divorce is going quite smoothly. I've never seen him this loose, this young. And before tonight I have no memory of him single as an adult. The power couple approaches the pool table and my brother breaks. His mouth slightly open, a wink to Anna, and he crushes the balls. Two stripes fall in.

"Ooh, I like my new partner," Anna says.

I envision a wedding, my brother and Anna running through an arc of pool cues, rice in the air.

Someone in the back of the bar yells my name but it's not for me. I try to find the artist but don't see him. The bar gets crowded. I think of my kids at home. Cam is far from done. I step outside and glance at the moon. A fingernail sliver but still bright enough to glow. Herb appears behind me and slaps my shoulder. He tells a knock-knock joke. I say, "Who's there?" without thinking. The punch line is "Morgan Freeman." I don't get it.

I walk back in and see Cam and Anna in the corner of the bar. She's on his lap and talking into his ear. They laugh, they coo, they may do it right here.

"I think I'm gonna head out," I say.

"We're moving on to a party," my brother says. "It's at Anna's beach house."

"Yeah, not me. It's almost ten."

"It's early."

"I think I'm out," I say. "Got kids home alone."

"Anna says it's Veterans Day," he says. "No school tomorrow."

The divorcé has parenting advice for me. "Next time," I say.

"Please," he says. "Please don't leave me tonight."

"I've gotta run," I yell over the music. "You know my address, right?"

"Don't go!"

"I've got kids at home."

"Yeah, one of 'em's fourteen years old."

"Thirteen."

"Stay. I love you man."

He loves me. I have to laugh.

"Please come back to my house," Anna says to me. "Come for an hour. Come on, let's get out of here."

I leave three messages on my son's phone, a text, and an email. Herb is behind me with his hands on my shoulders, just giddy with the prospect of a party, more free booze. I look around for my new best friend, the ponytailed painter. I don't see him. Cam and Anna start to leave and ten to twelve people follow them out. I'm in my car with Cam, Anna, Herb, and two women who resemble Anna in at least five ways. Her house is on the beach in Pass-a-Grille, not far past the toll plaza at Eckerd College. The smell of the salty gulf air is soothing. I call my son again and leave a last message. "Be home soon, decided to follow Uncle Cam to a party at the beach."

The house is enormous, bigger than even Teri's place. A mansion on the sand. I stand on Anna's deck and listen to the waves crash.

"She has foosball!" Herb yells. "Cam! Cam!"

My brother comes flying down the staircase in a fur hat with earflaps. "And a bidet!"

He and Herb high-five and head to the kitchen.

"Beer and wine in the fridge," says Anna.

People keep arriving. I see faces I know from the kids' school. And there she is, Teri, Ginger's mom. She doesn't see me yet. I grab a beer and plan to act surprised when she notices me. Cam is walking upstairs with Anna's hand in his. I think of his wife, then of his mistress.

"Hi Jay," Teri says.

"Wow, hi, didn't see you. Hi there, Teri," I say.

"Hey," she says, and gives me a hug. "Coincidence. Nice to see you! Is your wife here?"

I shake my head. "Business trip. Nice to see you too."

"Did you know that someone just went upstairs with Anna Montgomery?" she says.

There's no way I'm telling her it's my brother. She'll know soon enough. We stand outside and take in the ocean air.

I remember her easy beauty, the sensuality in the shape of her eyes. I remember our shoulders bumping and the way her lips moved as she spoke. I remember fearing our privacy and drinking more than my share.

I remember leaving alone.

Hangover

"What time did you get home? Daddy? Dad? Daddy?"

"I need to sleep a little more."

"Mom called last night and I told her you were out with your brother drinking beer. I left you a note, did you see it?"

"No."

"Where's Uncle Cam?"

"He's . . . at a hotel."

"But his suitcase is here."

"I'm sure he has other clothes."

"Why would he have other clothes?"

"I need to sleep a little more."

"Mom called three times this morning too. I told her you were asleep."

"Okay."

"She really wants to talk to you. She sounds upset."

I lift my phone and check. Five calls from my wife. I call her and she picks up on the second ring.

"I think I'm leaving this company," she says. "Where have you been, Jay?"

"With Cam."

"Cam is in Florida?"

She listens to my story. I listen to hers. She says she heard rumors there's trouble, layoffs, changes in company direction. "The air is getting thinner for me."

The shit and the fan will meet. We've been through this. It was years before we left San Francisco. There was a merger; she was asked to join the new company but it didn't interest her. She resisted and opted to quit with a severance. The vague and painful end of a startup she'd helped build was taxing. I became the breadwinner. And then we got pregnant.

"I'm sorry, Jackie," I say.

"I'll try to save it. But I have to go to LA for two nights," she says. "I'll know more then, and be home after that."

When I hang up I tell my daughter about the business trip. She goes into her *Les Misérables* face, a pauper girl in rags, her mother so far away. Alex walks in and I tell him about LA, two more nights. He grinds his jaw while dialing his mother. He leaves the room to talk. "I need you here," I hear him say. "No. Just come home, Mom."

He streams past me, handing the phone to his sister. I wait for his door to slam. *SLAM!*

"Hi, Mommy," Tara says and puts the phone on speaker.

"Hi, little girl."

"I miss you."

"I miss you too. I have such a crazy, big job," Jackie says. "It's one of the reasons we can say yes to so many things. You're also so lucky to have such a great daddy. I know so many families that have two parents working and the kids stay with a nanny or the grandma. So we get to say yes to things and we have Daddy. We're lucky."

When we hang up Tara watches TV and I head up to Alex's room. I knock and wait. No response. I crack the door open. He's on his bed, facedown. I sit on the edge and rest my hand on his back. I expect him to stop me, to shoo me away.

"Can I ask you a question?" I say.

He sniffs but doesn't move or speak.

"Do you love me?" I say, and regret the question. I await an answer anyway. When it doesn't come, I kiss the back of his head. And leave him be.

Tara and I watch the weather; another storm, they say, this one named Louisa. I will buy sandbags and maybe a canoe. A commercial comes on for laser vasectomies. The testimonials are convincing, with men stating they were on the table for fifteen minutes and came out sterile, unable to ever procreate again. When Tara leaves the room I'm on the phone, calling the number on the screen. 1-800-GOOD-BYE-SPERM. A voice mail picks up. I leave a message.

"I'd like to learn more," I say, and leave my address for a brochure.

🦋　　🦋　　🦋

In the morning I drive the kids to school. Tara tallies the hours left until Mommy's return. Alex has his earbuds in. I hear muffled rapping and a metallic drumbeat. His eyes appear glassy, distant. His mouth is locked closed, seemingly unable to open or lift from either corner. I think to tickle him to see if his smile even works. But it's a bad idea. I might never live it down. The kids get out of the car and I see Tara join her group of friends. A literal circle of little girls in green tops and khaki skirts. Alex walks through the many pods of cliques, acknowledging no one as he moves inside the building. I stare at him, ache for him, envision an embrace that wouldn't help him.

A car horn blasts behind me, *HONK!!!* I look in my rearview mirror and see my brother in the passenger seat. He's wailing on the horn, honking over and over, leaning over Anna to get my attention. I wave out my window. Cam's got his head out now — "Hey, you! Stop that guy! Hey, you!"

I pull over so he'll stop humiliating me. Anna is laughing, Cam is still barking. "Hey you!"

"Okay, stop that."

They're both flush with joy and impromptu sex, their true ages lost in the bounce of their giddy grins.

"What happened to you last night?" Anna asks, her mouth wide enough for me to count teeth.

"I had to get home. My wife is away and . . ."

"Your friend Herb woke up in the hot tub." They both laugh, recalling the most epic night in years.

"Yeah, I can picture that."

"We're praying he's gone when we get back," says Cam. "Listen, I need to get my stuff. I'm going to stay with Anna for a few days."

He glances at her. She looks down at her lap, trying not to boil over.

"Okay," I say.

"So I'll be by later. Around six. Anna's taking me around St. Pete today. You want to join us?"

"I have a job interview," I say.

"Really?" he says. "Doing what?"

"What do you mean, 'doing what'? I'm a copywriter, Cam. Remember? The job is for a copywriter."

"Yeah, yeah, I knew that. But I thought Jackie worked and you took care of the kids."

I look at Anna. "Well, we might switch," I say. "We're thinking of switching."

"Too bad. I'm here in town and you can't be with me."

"Call me later," I say. "Thanks for the invitation."

"Come by the house tonight," Anna yells. "I'm having a few friends over for a barbecue. Bring nothing but yourself. And the kids of course."

Cam nods. "I want to spend time with my niece and nephew," he says and sips from his coffee. Liar.

"Call me when you want to get your suitcase," I say.

I pull away and he starts honking again. "Hey you!" he yells. "Hey, I know that guy, that's my little brother!"

In my rearview I see him beaming, pointing at my car, a reborn child in the passenger seat. I think of his wife, then his mistress. And why I lied about the interview.

Dollhouse

Cam hasn't come to get his suitcase. I put it in the garage. Metaphorically I attempt to do the same with his divorce, the tsunami of his actions. After all, it's a new day. Up early, I feel charged, even invigorated. My amazing wife whom I will never, ever cheat on will be home within forty-eight hours and I want the house to shine. I have dishes to do, beds to make, laundry to run.

I head out for coffee but decide to buy flowers instead. She'll be drained from flying and the cryptic and passive-aggressive facial expressions of her coworkers. Overworked and overplucked, she just needs to be able to recognize herself in the reflection of us, our home. The flowers in the grocery store are a light purple with little yellow flames on the inside of each petal. I buy them and also some salmon, salad, and asparagus. Ben and Jerry's Heath Bar Crunch for dessert. I marinate and grill salmon well and will surprise her with this dish, one of her favorites. My daughter hates fish, I remember too late, so I buy her a dollhouse I see in the window of an antique store. It's old and beat up but doesn't have mold, so I'll propose we ditch the Barbie Dreamhouse, call this fixer-upper an art project, and paint, sand, and remodel any part of it she wants. I'm the smartest father of a little girl in the universe. In two more years she'll be twelve and laugh at me—a dollhouse, an art project with my dad? No *way*. But today I have her. As if digging a ditch, I break ground on a memory that will never, ever leave her.

I'm at the school early in anticipation of revealing the gift. I see my girl, running among the other blondies, her backpack bouncing up and down, her tongue out for emphasis. She gets in the car and I give her a long hug. She pivots her head, worried other kids will see her getting squeezed.

"Stop, Daddy."

"I bought you something today."

"Really? What?"

"It's for you and me to do together. A project."

"What is it?"

"Guess."

"No drama, Daddy. I had the worst day."

"Okay, okay, you got it out of me. It's a dollhouse."

"I don't like dollhouses."

"Oh. Well. I'll just have to work on it alone."

"You're not a girl!"

"Boys can play with dollhouses."

"You're not a boy either."

"Maybe Mom will like it."

"When is she home?"

"Tomorrow night."

I see Alex, seated alone among his classmates. I lower my window and call his name. When he hears it, he looks at me horrified, walks our way.

"Did you have to yell?" he asks. The first question he's asked me in two days.

"Sorry. I just needed you to see me."

A song I like comes on the radio. AC/DC. I turn it louder.

"I love this song," I say. "It's called 'Have a Drink on Me.'"

"I hate this song," my daughter says.

"Oh, come on."

"Please turn that horrible music off!" she yells.

"Do you like it, Alex? The rock 'n' roll, boogie-woogie blues?"

In the rearview I see him nod. He likes it. A nod from Alex is the equivalent of leaping like a pogo stick for most humans. He likes it. I make it slightly louder and bounce my head to the beat.

"Lower the music!" Tara yells.

So I do.

"I do *not* want to hear that music."

"But Alex does. Right, buddy?"

My cell phone rings.

"Hello?"

"This is Dr. Jacobs' office, returning your call."

"Oh, I'm sorry," I say, "which doctor? Eyes, teeth, or regular?"

"No, sir. Dr. Jacobs is a urologist. We assumed from your message that you were interested in getting information on the process of a vasectomy."

Vasectomy. I feel this word in my testicles.

"Oh, yes. This is he," I say. "I am me. I mean, I called. About that . . . topic. Hello?"

Going Solo

| *Cloudy with a rough wind, sailboats teetering*

Tara howls with glee when her mother walks in the door. She caught an earlier flight. We thought she'd be home at nine but she's here at six. My daughter receives her seventh snow globe, this one of the Hollywood sign, floating in rainbow glitter. She's so happy, bouncing from wall to wall, so much to say. Alex's gift is a watch. His first real timepiece. Jackie calls his name but he doesn't respond.

"Mommy, listen to this," Tara says. "Ginger and I decided to let Marie into our group because, I don't know if you know Marie but she's a little weird—not weird, but more smart, maybe, but she's really not having any luck finding a best friend. So Marie is now Ginger's and my best friend too."

"That's so thoughtful, baby; I'm so proud of you for looking out for her."

"Yeah, I'm doing more of that now. We hang out under the jungle gym? In a place no boys can go? Unless they want to get teased? We hide there after lunch, just before PE. This boy Jimmy . . . ?"

I follow them up to our bedroom with Jackie's suitcase in hand. The stories continue in a barrage of questions that aren't questions. My wife laughs, shows surprise, kisses her girl, assures her she's being heard by repeating details: "Five girls under one slide?" Jackie knocks on Alex's door. No response. She tries the knob. Locked.

"Sissy Kramer's mom came to class and we made real piggy banks? Out of clay? And I'm so, so, so, so excited to show you mine but it has to stay in the kiln."

"Alex, baby," Jackie says, knocking. "I got you something good. Open up. Why isn't your brother opening his door?"

"He never does," says Tara. "My bank is a reddish pink because it's a piggy bank. Pigs are pink, so mine is pink. Ginger went with yellow. You have to see it, Mama."

"Alex!?" she says and knocks louder. Nothing.

"Alex!" I yell the loudest. Enough of this. I walk up and pound on the door with my arm. We wait. Jackie looks at me. What the fuck.

"Alex!" I say, and my forearm hammers his door. "*Alex!*"

Nothing. My mind plays tricks and the fear is dizzying. He's asleep, my son is napping and it's time to wake him up. I take two steps back and prepare to plow my right shoulder into his door.

"Jay, wait," Jackie says.

"Daddy, don't," says Tara.

"*Stop!*" Alex barks from inside. My heart. He unlocks the door but doesn't open it. My wife doesn't flinch, just steps in his room and closes the door behind her. Tara and I look at each other. I can feel my heartbeat in my eyes, the back of my neck. Tara and I go in my room and wait. She picks up her story where she left off.

"I have to tell Mommy this too. Jenny McMurphy's sister Lulu is treasurer of our school. She was elected. That means everyone voted for her. Well, not everyone. But she won."

He's got us on eggshells. His temperament rules, has us scattering to appease. In my mind he heard me, the knocking, the screaming of his name. Whether he was sleeping or faking, brooding or stewing, I'm starting to resent the fear. The corner he's shoved me into. Patience is always the key to good parenting. That extra deep breath. But I almost want to kick his door down right now. Wake up, man, life is only going to get steeper and one day I won't be there to be so fucking patient.

". . . so many more colors of fish than I have because her fish tank is for saltwater fish only."

"Saltwater?"

"Yup."

I hear Alex's door open and Jackie calmly enters our bedroom.

"What did he say?" I ask.

"Nothing, really. He put the watch on. Looks nice on him. I think he likes it."

"I mean, why did he ignore us?"

"I think he was sleeping. Okay. I need both of you to help me with something," she says. She opens her suitcase and pulls out a dress. "I found this in LA. It's for an event I have in two weeks. You have to be honest when I put it on, okay? Tell me if it's too . . . ya know . . . anything. Too whatever."

She disappears into her closet and my daughter continues. "Mommy, Ginger's mother puts on dresses for us and says the same thing."

"How is Ginger?"

"She's fine. Her mom wants me to help plan her birthday. We're thinking bowling for now but Ginger keeps saying she wants to roller-skate. We may need to rethink it."

"Either way it'll be fun. Now, don't react right away. Just take a second." My wife walks out in a black formal dress, long to the ground, and sparkly high heels. She spins, gorgeous, the zipper down in the back.

"It's so beautiful, Mommy!"

It is. For the moment she is the only person on my mind. "It's very pretty on you," I say. I zip the zipper and dip my head to kiss her shoulder. The dress, perfect on her frame, is like butter to the touch. We slow-dance to no music, our daughter the ideal third wheel. The dress will not be worn for me, as I am not invited to the ball. It is an inside event, a prom for Jackie and the other employees of her company. The truth that I will not be permitted to stand next to my own wife as she models this gorgeous dress isn't sitting well. I plop on the end of the bed, absorbing the silent weight of my realization. My wife and daughter dance and spin, dip and laugh. The hem around the bottom of the dress flows loosely along with them and I am taunted now by the fabric, the silky cloth not meant for me at all.

"Too bad I won't be there."

"I know," she says. "I hate going to these things without you."

"No, you don't."

She stops and stares. She looks down at her daughter, still clamped to her waist. "Why is Daddy so silly?"

My daughter shrugs. "Maybe he wants to be invited to fun things too."

I point at Tara. "I just wish I got to spend as much time with you as some of the men at your company."

"Stop that bull. I fought my way home to see you," she says.

"I know."

"You hate these events."

"All I'm saying is you look like a party of one. In a gorgeous dress. You look available."

"Available?"

"That's probably the wrong word."

"Can you please be quiet?" our daughter says.

My wife reaches for her zipper. "For a writer you say the wrong word a lot. Did you know that?"

"I never said I was a good writer."

She mock laughs. "You said that, not me."

"Who's going to zip you up on the night of the bash?"

"Stop that. You're being antagonistic."

"Because I wish my wife was home more?"

"If you think I'm interested in someone other than you, then you're the one with the problem. Not me."

"This is a very stupid conversation," Tara says.

"I agree," I say.

"Good," my wife says. "Let's stop."

I walk out of the room and pass Alex's door. My instinct's to keep moving but I find myself knocking again. "Can I speak to you, please?"

My wife pokes her head out of the bedroom. "He's studying."

"I just want to talk to him for a second."

The door unlocks and opens. Alex is livid, his jaw leading the rage. "What?"

His emotion can come only through his face, his eyes, a slouch in his right hip. He has no time for me, his father, the person who wiped his tush and sang him to sleep for years, kissing his soft head. Now I'm just the guy to ignore, to avoid, to shoo away. I'm the person pictured under *Father* in all the Freudian textbooks. Team Oedipus. Enemy number one. The task is to draw from intelligence, experience, to giggle it away and prepare for hindsight, a time when even Alex has forgotten these long minutes of excruciating angst. One day, with his daughter on his lap, he'll laugh with us, recall those tricky transitional years. I am him, he is me.

"I need to say something," I say.

"So say it," he says.

My words, my tone, my presence exhaust him. I remember my father's need for distance too. So much he left and never looked back. Our family mantra was that we didn't need him. Cam saw him as dead and used to draw pictures of caskets. The word *Dad* on the side. My mother painted him as a criminal of soul, a man without empathy. Who has children and lets them fall away?

Alex begins to shut the door. I stop it with my shoe.

"I'd like to be alone." he says.

"Can we talk?"

"I'm studying,"

I'm a gear he can manipulate. A constant as he maneuvers among the haze. But right about now, I don't react like someone with insight. Right about now I instead lose the reins. In this moment I attempt to express, to find my way through the knot in my chest. But it will be remembered only as the day Daddy went too far, said too much, abandoned the most crucial precept in the art of healthy parenting: *never become the child. The child needs you to remain the adult. Wait. Breathe. Think. React.*

Dr. Ron Zinnman

MONDAY | *Not in the mood*

Alex sits across from me in the therapist's office. His shoulders are forward, his fingers clasped. The doctor is letting the silence work for him, for us. All we can do is review the moment when I snapped and get to a point where I can apologize in earnest. He addresses me first, wants to know the message I was trying to deliver. He'd of course like me to do it without hollering, flailing, name calling, or kicking. He'd like me to try to express myself without destroying anything, like the banister on our staircase.

"What happened, Jay?"

"I lost my temper."

"Okay. Do you remember why?"

"Yes."

"Who did you lose your temper with?"

"My son."

"Tell me why."

"It doesn't matter. I am to blame. I am the adult. It just got away from me."

"What did? What got away from you?"

"My control."

"And how did that manifest itself to Alex?"

"I yelled at him."

"Did you scare him?"

"I don't know. Probably."

I look at my son. His lowered head is shaking, no. "You didn't scare me," he says.

"I acted like a jerk. Out of control."

"You called me names," Alex says. "What kind of father calls his son names?"

"I'm sorry, Alex. I acted stupidly."

"Yeah, stupidly," he says.

"Okay," Dr. Zinnman says. "What were the names you called Alex?"

"Just idiotic things. I wasn't even thinking when I said them. I was out of my head with anger."

"Do you remember what your dad called you, Alex?"

Alex reaches for the floor plant. He digs his fingernail into the body of a leaf. "Dullard."

I look at the doctor, embarrassed. I'm a child. In a man's body. He doesn't look back at me.

"Okay, any other things, other names?"

Alex is thinking.

"I said parenting was thankless."

"Okay, thankless. Anything else?"

"Yes," says Alex. "There were more."

"I think I called him a sad sack and a wet blanket."

The doctor nods and writes this down. "Anything else?"

"I think that's it," I say.

Silence.

Three minutes, four minutes. I am a moron.

"Alex? Would you like to say something to your father? Something about what happened the other night?"

"No."

"Do you think your father acted inappropriately?"

"I think he always acts inappropriately."

"Always?"

He nods.

"In what way does your father act inappropriately?"

He shrugs, reaches for the plant. "He's always trying to be my buddy or whatever. I'm not his buddy. He's always trying to hug me, like, reaching out to me, and I don't like it. I don't want to be squeezed like a stupid little baby. He makes me feel like a stupid little baby."

I can't help but stare at him. I stop, look at my hands.

"How do you react to that, Jay?"

"I am surprised. Surprised to hear he feels that way. I know he's furious with me. I can see that, feel that. I understand I'm to blame."

"Let's veer from blame. I just want to hear your thoughts."

"Oh, okay. Um, I raised him. Hands on, ya know. I was the hired nanny, only these were my own kids. I used to rely on the word *selflessness*. I felt like I had a true grasp of it and it would guide my parenting. This one word. I'd pat myself on the back for understanding it so fully. It meant being home, being ready for their needs. It meant loving them, in all aspects. Being a mom and a dad."

Dr. Ron is writing, nodding.

"But I guess I failed, somewhere. Because of his temperament, the moods, the day in, day out of the way he sees me, looks at me. I can't . . . find the selflessness right now. I can't apply it to Alex because when I try to hone in on it, I'm left with a sense of disrespect that begs me to protect my own honor, I guess. The result is selfishness. It feels selfish. In its rawest form."

"Alex?"

He looks up at the doctor.

"What do you think of what your father just said? Do you hear him? Does it resonate with you?"

Alex never looks at me. He shifts in his seat, reaches for the leaf.

"No."

"No, it doesn't resonate with you?"

"No. I wasn't listening."

I look at the doctor. He looks at me.

"Alex, I'd like to talk to your dad alone for a moment. Do you mind going in the waiting room with your mom for a minute or two?"

Alex stands slowly and leaves the room. I shut my eyes and let the warmth of the gently lit room engulf my achy head.

"How do you feel?" the doctor asks.

"Uh. A little worn out."

"Yes, I understand. I want to take a second and explain the teenage brain to you," he says. He offers me a model of the brain. I take it from him and it falls into two pieces in my hands.

"It's okay, it's suppose to do that. Now look. In adults, various parts of the brain work together to evaluate choices, make decisions, and act accordingly in each situation. The teenage brain doesn't appear to work like this. For comparison's sake, think of the teenage brain as an entertainment center that hasn't been fully hooked up. There are loose wires, so that the speaker system isn't working with the DVD player, which in turn hasn't been formatted to work with the TV yet. And to top it all off, the remote control hasn't even arrived."

My laugh comes through my nose.

"I tell parents this analogy all the time because it's crucial you understand that the cards are stacked against you for the next seven years. Maybe less, maybe more. Good parenting can't stop what's going on in your house. But it will help when he's ready to reenter the world as a fully functional person. You were right about self-lessness. It's just way harder to locate and utilize when your son is seemingly ignoring you, making you feel shitty with every glance."

The doctor is waiting, staring, now leaning forward to touch my knee. "I think you're doing a great job. And like I've said before, and I know you and Jackie have trepidation, I do recommend an antidepressant for Alex. He deserves a boost when it comes to his serotonin level. We're adding nothing to his brain chemistry. All we'd be doing is recharging the mechanism that already exists. The advances in these medicines have been remarkable in the last ten years. I believe he's a great candidate. So, discuss it again, research a few of them. Celexa, Wellbutrin, maybe Prozac. Just read about them for now, and let me know your thoughts. Do you have any questions for me?"

I can hardly move. My legs feel like logs.

"Yes."

"Fire away," he says.

"Is it genetic? Depression?"

He nods, with an apologetic smile. "Have you suffered from it?"

I nod.

"Wanna talk about it?"

I sit taller and look at Alex's empty seat. I check my watch. "I think I have daddy issues."

Sock Hop

FRIDAY | *Drizzle, blue, drizzle*

Cam calls. He says, good news, his ex will allow Kimmy to join us for Thanksgiving. I smile, thinking of seeing her at my mom's home. He then adds, "for twelve thousand dollars in cash." My mother has already asked him if he'll pay the ridiculous sum. Cam is angry at her for wanting him to consider it. Thanksgiving is the holiday my mother loves the most. I anticipate a house filled with family and feel heartache for my niece, the little girl who will be missing.

Ray and Ray's daughter Katrina have celebrated the day with us before. She isn't my mother's granddaughter but she's a warm, sweet body. I'm over the stupid birthday night. I call him and he's surprised to hear from me. He says he hasn't seen Katrina in two weeks because Lizzie took her to Atlanta. Why Atlanta? He says Lizzie has cousins there. I ask if he can try to get her for the holiday. He says he'll try. When I ask about his health, his state of mind, he says he's going to take classes in business, architecture, and engineering at an online college with a name he's forgetting momentarily. He wonders if I'd be interested in helping him pay for it. I tell him we can talk about it when I see him. Ugh.

When I hang up I have a message from the kids' school. Oh no. I envision the woods in the back. Alex has begun a cult and they slaughtered a sheep near the football field. I call back and get Judith Margolis, the vice principal.

"Yes," she says, "I was looking for you. Sock hop is Tuesday. Would it be possible for you or your wife to help us transport five cocktail tables and their stems to the school by five p.m. tomorrow?"

I'm so relieved. Thank God it's not about Alex. "My wife is traveling."

"We got ourselves in a lurch here because our volunteer had a family emergency."

"Oh."

"It's for the sock hop. The fund-raiser. I'm sure you were planning on coming anyway."

I grip the bridge of my nose and squeeze with my eyes closed. "Yes. I can do it. Where do I pick them up?"

🐦   🐦   🐦

Tara and I find the rental place. The tables are ready to go. They ask me to sign, I do, and we get it all to the school. Teri and Ginger are there, setting up the balloons and streamers, the DJ stuff, these cardboard moons and planets. Teri works with amazing vigor, pointing both arms, answering questions, patting an enormous delivery guy on the back for bringing the right glassware. Tara and Ginger run off to their lockers and Teri hands me a list of tasks and pats me on the back too. There are twenty or more tables in the "little theater" that need to be in the gym by tomorrow. She points out that not only am I present, but so is Herb. He and I start lifting rectangular tables one by one and leaning them beneath the basketball hoop. After a while one of the PE teachers helps us. I'm sweating, my muscles firing, and it feels pretty good. Teri is appreciative; her pupils sparkle. The setup goes so quickly, we end up celebrating back at Herb's. He has a trampoline, a boat, a pool in the shape of a lotus flower, and a yellow Lab. He makes margaritas and I'm buzzing after one. When I find Teri, Herb is telling her a story about the day he bought his boat. She reacts with generosity, her attention all his.

"Really," she says. "You truly got the price down by telling the salesman you knew Jack Nicholson?"

Yawn. The whole bullshit tale is meant to impress her, to get her all randy for Herb, the most bloated armchair sailor in Florida. I'm jealous. So stupid. Of Herb. Like so many men I see down here, Herb's replaced any attempt at personal attractiveness with boats and real estate. Cash makes up for everything for certain women. Five-foot-deep navel? No problem, where's the credit card? Cigarette halitosis and visible earwax? No worries, today I'm buying shoes made of lemur feet.

"So I says to the guy, I says, 'You got a job to do, I got a job to do, and Uncle Sam's got a job to do to both of us. I can see right away, because I've been in sales for thirty-two years, that his eyes are with me; ya know, the eyes never lie. You got extremely pretty eyes.'"

"Thanks, Herb," says Teri, a quick lift of her shoulders.

"So I got this idiot on the hook, right?" Herb has his finger in his mouth, yanking on his inner cheek, fish on. "Oh, no," he says, mumbling, drawing a huge smile from Teri. "I knew I had him. Yank, yank, yank. I ended up getting a fifty-foot yacht for less than half the asking. You want to go sit on her? I call her *Smooth Groove*."

Her head cranes to me, eyebrows high, pleading: Don't leave me alone with Herb, please.

"Can we all see the boat?" I ask.

So all of us, the kids, the parents drinking margaritas, we all watch the sunset from the back of Herb's boat. He plays the kids' favorite tunes on the radio and we get loose as the colors off Tampa Bay begin to shock and awe. Purples dart through burnt oranges and liquid blues. Sea greens arrive as if in a painter's design, from horizon to water and up again. The whirl of the light show is unprecedented for me, the trails and sparks, the sunset a flower. I feel stronger, like myself for the moment. Did I just see a fish jump clean out of the water? I grab my daughter and plant my lips against her right cheek. I smell her quickly and let her squirm away. "Get off me, Daddy."

Teri finds my affection quite sweet. She uses the words *tender dad*. It's as if my brain's been released, given some free time in the yard. Maybe I am a good dad. Teri leaves the captain's chair and plants herself next to me. Nicki Minaj moans nasally from the radio as Herb hands me a fresh drink. I tell him I better stop. He calls me a pussy. I take the drink from him and Teri suggests we split it. She takes the first sip, a hardy one, and then hands it to me. Our bare forearms touch and I almost say, "I like your skin." I keep the words inside my brain. I tell her I've drunk enough.

"Daddy, dolphins!"

"No way," I say, but there they are, about five.

We all head to the front of the vessel. Herb asks if we should chase them and Ginger and Tara say, "No," at the same time. Let's not go anywhere. There's no reason to. Herb jogs to the captain's seat and grabs his binoculars. Placing them firmly against his eyes, he assesses the situation.

"Just what I thought," he announces. "Bottlenose. They're heading up the gulf to feed."

Teri whistles softly to the dolphins, as if they're dogs. I feel her head on my shoulder.

Herb faces us with the binoculars and says, "Oh."

Tara and Ginger look at us.

And Teri lifts her head.

Meeting of the Minds

SATURDAY | *Starry night*

Jackie's decided to keep loving me. It was a tight contest but I squeaked out a victory. Name calling and broken railing aside, my marriage still has legs. The doghouse is a lonely place. I overcompensate with my son, envisioning myself immune to his contempt. I smile with warmth when I pass him and attempt to evoke a silent air of approachability. I find him alone at the kitchen table, pondering a brochure for a school retreat to Key West. All I want to do is read it with him. I say nothing. Give him the space he deserves. I make a bowl of cereal and sit at the table. The back of the brochure has photos of dolphins and teal-hued stingray pools. A bird's-eye view of the campus suggests remarkable beauty, the edge of the earth, an aquatic wonderland.

"Man, are you gonna have fun on this trip."

He looks up at me as if my voice is a car alarm. I'm still smiling, but also chewing cereal. The crunch, perhaps the slurp of the milk is irritating. He stands with his literature and leaves the room.

I find Jackie in our bedroom. She says Alex is showing zero interest in leaving town, bunking with classmates, buying water shoes, or relinquishing his phone during daytime hours. I tell her I'd love to discuss it with him but my instincts suggest I move to the moon instead.

Jackie calls her father to remind him about Thanksgiving. He asks if he can bring a date. My wife asks me if I think my mother would mind another guest, a woman her father is courting. I call my mother to ask. She picks up and she's off, carrying the phone down the stairs to a filing cabinet. I hear her open it, the shuffling papers.

"Jackie told me about Alex and his doctor's thoughts about antidepressants. I want you to try Celexa. I have multiple patients on it and there are few to no side effects. Have you heard of that one?"

"Yes, Mom. That's the one we're going with. It's important you not bring it up at the Thanksgiving table."

"Do you honestly think I'd do that?"

"No, of course not."

"Should I expect Ray and Katrina?"

"I haven't heard back. Just expect them."

"What's the woman's name?"

"Who?"

"The woman coming with Jackie's dad?"

"I don't know."

"Find out. I'm making name tags."

I hang up and Teri calls, wanting to know if we want to have dinner before the sock hop.

"Maybe, let me ask Jackie. You up for dinner with Teri and Ginger before the sock hop tonight?"

My wife stares at me, in a doghouse-type way.

"We're going to Troy Young's house for a party tonight. I've told you about it for two weeks."

I put my hand over the phone. I tell her the sock hop is a big deal, that I helped set up chairs and tables with Herb and that Teri is expecting us.

"Who's Teri?"

"Ginger's mother."

"You begged me to invite you to the next work party. Remember?"

"I have a dilemma," I tell Teri. "I'll call you back."

I hang up and my wife takes my face in her hands. "Troy's house. Tonight. You're coming with me. Think of it as duty calls. We are a family that is searching for peace. It's just one night."

        🎜   🎜   🎜

Troy's been in the gaming business since the early seventies, back when arcade machines were only found in bars and game rooms. Today the company puts out seventy-two titles, including certain war games that make as much money as blockbuster films.

We arrive a little early, my tie too tight. Troy answers the door wearing a black kilt and carrying a plastic sword to honor his new 3-D game, *Scotsman's Reign*. His voice is more like that of a dosed Liza Minnelli than a Scotsman when he announces things like, "Caviar, bitches!" His signature full head of white hair and traffic-cone skin are legendary. I'm offered champagne by a male server in a very tight T-shirt. I try to enjoy the spectacle. I like the wacky bathrooms with gold toilet seats and infinity pool bidets. This is probably my third time here for dinner since we arrived in Florida. Most of the other guests are top-tier executives like my wife, and their spouses. It's a dinner party, which at Troy's house means an additional eight male waiters, all with Paul Newman's chin and thick calves. The hired women are gorgeous too. They merely dole out sashimi and then dumplings filled with lamb. I get a drink and begin to meander. Three times around the pool. I know that guy.

"Hi, yes, I know you, sure, from Troy's last soiree."

I drink another short glass of tequila and look for my wife. There she is. Talking, putting that long piece of hair of hers behind her ear. She's the most attractive woman in the room, especially amid all the rhinoplasty. As I approach her circle I get a kiss on the cheek, an introduction, some kudos for my hair, my height. My wife is told she's lucky, to have such a supportive, handsome husband.

"Yes," she says, and I sense a tinge of sarcasm. She sees me read it wrong and I get another kiss before sauntering away. I land by the ice sculpture of the company logo, next to the spouse of one of the board members. I've met her before. Greta Holmes. She must be eighty but her face is yanked back into a Terry Gilliam wet dream. I do all I can to avoid staring at the exposed insides of her eyelids, which have chunky black makeup mixed in. It's like something out of a Bela Lugosi film. She takes a faux sip of her wine by bumping her overblown lips against the rim of the glass.

"How you liking Florida? Love it?"

"It's fine. I think . . ."

"Love it, right? How are you treating that gorgeous wife of yours? She's a queen."

"I . . ."

"Don't you ever let her get away. She is smarter than anyone I know about computers, technology. She is a rock star. Without her we'd sink. The company needs her. She knows where the company must go in the new age. Let me tell ya something, it's Greek to me."

"Me too."

"But she's special; we need her, more than you know. And she's a mother, my God. I have no idea how she does it all."

"When we first met . . ."

"I couldn't do it," Greta says. "I was unable to raise kids and work at the same time. I had to hire a nurse and when my kids got older they told me I wasn't really their mother because Maria was their mother. That's who raised them. They tell me this now. It's awful to hear, from your children. I didn't know how much I was hurting them."

She bumps her glass to her lips.

I drink my tequila too fast. Gone. I find myself trying to suck the booze from the ice, mining the cubes for an eyedropperful more.

"Looks like you need another, sailor," Greta says, flirting with me. From the corner of my eye I see her pose, sort of, the way she did for actual sailors in 1968.

I drink the next glass too fast too. What the hell, they're free.

Greta sticks with me and it's fine, the woman's without boundaries and it can be hilarious. We get to the bar just in time for shots of something brown. I bow out and Greta laughs and goes into a wobbly story about meeting Wallace Stegner. A coding guy named George joins us. He's got a thick red ponytail that ends in the middle of his back. Another man who looks like Dick Van Dyke but with Frankenstein's browridge tells us through a German accent that he "vasn't expecting so much teets 'n' ahss." I guess he isn't used to the way the wealthy party in St. Pete. I tell him who's who, pointing out Troy and Marjorie Dillman, my wife's assistant. And look, it's Gary Fry. Gary has teeth that can be seen from Neptune. He's always at these gatherings and always with a different blond teenager.

Rumor has it he "did *it*" with Donna Summer on Karl Lagerfeld's yacht in Portofino. He waves to people he's not next to and hugs those he's near. Troy sees Gary's arrival as a sign that it's dinnertime so in a surprisingly loud voice he tells us all to adjourn to the dining room. My nameplate has me next to Greta and her husband, a man who resembles Yogi Bear. I have no idea where my wife is.

"What line-a-work you in?" Yogi wants to know.

I wash and wrap heads of lettuce for Safeway. I evaluate the value of an evaluation and then assess the vagaries of the assumptions. I recall the calling cards of frequent callers. I taste-test for Play-Doh and Elmer's Glue. I am an exorcist. I am a novelist. I am a liar.

"I'm a novelist."

Even with my chin lowered into my tomato bisque, I can sense the heads turning. By saying *novelist* I've separated myself from those who dabble, those who blog, and those who studied English as undergrads. This is especially the case among guests so highly defensive of their cultural limitations.

"Might I have read your work?" asks an elderly man across the table.

"I'm not sure," I say.

"Do you mean it's out of print?"

I nod. "Oh, yes."

The reaction is a mix of relief and letdown. He is a writer, but it may not be worth telling anyone because his books are so obscure.

"How would I find your work?" the man asks.

"I don't know," I admit. "There aren't many bookstores."

"I have a friend who writes books," Marjorie says. "Do you know a book called *Long Acre Nights*?"

"It rings a bell," I say. But it doesn't.

I see my wife. She sits near me, absorbing the glances of my admirers. The dinner is pork tenderloin and I like the texture of it. The chef really nailed it. I tried it once on the grill for the kids and it came out too charred. My wife is telling a story to our corner of the table. It's about a job she had in San Francisco.

"I was seven months pregnant, had eleven minutes to get to the convention center at CES," she says, referring to the Consumer Electronics Show. "The cab driver says he knows another route so he's flying and I'm holding my belly and suddenly there's Donald Trump, just standing on the corner. My cab driver is blown away so he stops the cab to yell at Donald. I tell the guy I have two minutes to get to the Hilton. He says, 'Lady, it's the Donald.' He parks, gets out of the car. So I get out too, will have to find another taxi."

Oh, no. Not this story. It's about how she called me that very moment. I told her to put the cab driver on the phone, said I wanted to talk to him.

"So I go back and tell the guy my husband wants to talk to him."

There are some giggles from her audience.

"The driver, who is having tons of trouble getting anywhere near the Donald, takes the phone from my hand. And I watch his face as Jay talks to him. The man stares at me, looks at my belly, and blinks a million times before taking me by my elbow and guiding me back to his taxi."

There is some applause for me. "What did you say to him?" they want to know.

"Triplets," I say. "I told him she was having triplets."

Laughter: what a couple, what a team, how could anyone can a lady with a husband so sharp and witty? The night blurs from here, lots of laughing, loose lips, and for a while I escape it all, and sit alone in the den. My wife finds me. She says I was sleeping.

"No, I wasn't."

"Liar."

"Can you drive?" she asks.

I stand and flatten my bunched and starched shirt. I hand her the keys.

Troy is in the doorway. I realize thanking him for the evening will provoke more small talk. My mind says to feign sickness or something, anything to get past my glorious host. No dice. He embraces us both, again, and waits to hear the expected wows about the evening. Like the grand maestro he is, Troy may as well have a towel around his neck, bowing as he's handed a bouquet. He absorbs all twelve of the adjectives my wife finds to describe the party. Maybe we'll keep the job.

On the way to the car my wife has to vent all the shit she heard, overheard, wasn't supposed to hear but will be privy to at Friday's offsite. I can't believe so much negativity was swirling in there. I thought it was all cool, the triplets story, the way I did shots with Greta. It makes me nuts to hear that so much time was devoted to meanness. Corporate America, the roughest of all the contact sports. She still thinks she might be out. All that kissing and drinking and her job security is as flighty as Troy.

"I'm gonna go in there on Monday and try to sort it out," she says. "It's so fucking maddening. Everyone seems to have a different idea—they aren't even listening to one another."

"I'm really sorry," I say.

"I work so hard for them. I'm gonna go in there and ask in the nicest, most professional voice I can muster, what the hell is up?"

Jackie starts the car and pulls onto the street.

"It's time for that convention in Aspen again," she says. "I know, it sucks for us both, but I have to go a day early this year."

"I remember, three nights, you told me."

"Four nights, back before breakfast on the red-eye Friday. Tuesday I've got Samsung, Wednesday Facebook, Thursday Google, and then Troy is celebrating the launch of *Scotsman's Reign*."

I don't want to say anything. She'll look amazing again as she parties, listening to whoever the company hired to perform, the Foo Fighters or Method Man. Jackie pulls onto our street and into the driveway. She turns the car off and we sit for a moment in the dark, the radio silent. My wife yawns, rubs her left eyebrow. She hasn't been able to turn off since she left the house, eleven hours ago.

"The last thing I want to ask you tonight," she says.

I face her.

". . . is whether you're in the mood."

"For that?"

She climbs on top of me in the passenger seat and undoes my belt.

"I've been meaning to talk to you," I say.

"Can we talk afterwards?" She kisses me.

"I've been having some thoughts," I say.

"Me too. When's the last time we did it in a car?"

I don't want another baby. I already brought one into the world in pain.

"I don't think so," I say, but she doesn't hear me. We haven't done it in a car since Nantucket in 1989.

"Jackie?"

She tries to fire up the generator. She kisses me. "Come on, baby."

I try to get into the groove but my penis is sound asleep.

"Come on now," she says. "Come out and play with me."

It's not happening. Nothing is happening.

"I don't want another baby."

She freezes. "What'd you say?"

I sit there, her weight on me, the moonlight on her hair. "I don't . . . feel as if someone is missing from our dinner table."

Pause.

She jumps out of the car, slams the door behind her, and walks into the house. I follow her in and up the stairs. She's in the bathroom, the door locked.

"Jackie?"

She doesn't answer. I sit on the floor of our bedroom and knock with the back of my hand. "Hey, babe?"

"I need to be alone right now."

"I didn't mean to upset you."

Silence.

I knock again.

"Please," she says. "Just stop."

"I love our family with all that I am," I say.

She turns the sink on and lets it run.

As I doze off that night I begin to dream through a surface sleep. I'm on a subway in New York City. I look across the aisle and see myself in a pink maternity blouse. It has ruffles around the sleeves and neck and it's way too small. If I curve my shoulders inward I can tear a hole right down the back. My navel's exposed. A woman in a security guard uniform points at me and then all the people see my pink top. A construction worker, a little boy. I laugh too, trying to ease their discomfort. I wake up to feel my wife getting in bed.

"Hey," I say. "You okay?"

She rolls over, her back to me.

"I love you," I whisper.

She sighs.

The night is choppy, takes too long to end.

PART THREE

Thanksgiving

"Now boarding Elite, Platinum only. Please do not approach if you're not an Elite or Platinum United Club member."

Jackie's the only one in our family who's Elite. My boarding pass has a 9 on it, Section 9. You can't get farther from Elite than 9. There is no 10. This plane may very well leave without me.

Once we're seated, I lean in and get a kiss from my wife. Two days ago a kiss was still uncertain. Time is helping. We finally pull away from the airport but wait on the tarmac for an hour. I don't feel United in *any* way. We're headed to Newark and Newark is congested. I stew in the fact that, in her eyes, I am flaccid. You're only as good as your last at bat. The agony between opportunities to come through. It's this I see when I look at her. Flaccidity. No more babies.

Two and a half hours after we take off, we're in a holding pattern over Newark. We may never land. Until we do.

The table at my mother's house is in the shape of a giant L. Small clay turkeys with candles in each sit on orange, pilgrim-shaped doilies. The girls, Tara and Katrina, made the candleholders. My father-in-law is here with a woman he's dating. She says her name is Simka but the affected way she pronounces it makes me think she made it up: "I'm *Seem*-ka." I bet her name is Judy or Betty. I liked the last woman but thought the one before that wasn't funny enough for him. *Seem*-ka has the entitled air of an urbane social-ite and looks like a tall Kathy Griffin. Her handshake is more like a gift: here, take this, do what you will with it. Cam arrives with Anna and I watch my mother embrace her. I try to make Anna feel comfortable but she appears petrified, aware now that Cam's mother learned of the divorce only last week. I decide to take a break from the crowd and go smell my stepdad's pies, my mother's yams. I find Cam in the kitchen and he pulls me aside.

"I want you to tell Mom that you love Anna."

"That I *love* her?"

"Make sure Mom knows you think she's special. Get it?"

My father-in-law helps my stepfather, Roger, pull the turkey out of the oven and everyone claps and toasts and we drink wine and laugh louder than normal. I see Alex in glimpses. The earbuds always in, the hoodie always up. The new medicine is in his sys-tem, five days now. He's outside on the patio furniture, his phone in both hands. My daughter walks over to me as I watch Alex from the window. Her fingertips rub my back in circles. The love I feel is palpable, like a cartoon heart pounding from my chest. I hug her, my wineglass dangling. "Thanks," I say.

Ray sits next to us in the den. Katrina joins us too. She has a sock puppet on her right hand; it has googly eyes, yellow eyebrows made of felt. "My name is Lucy," the puppet says to me. "I'm a writer of great books."

"Hi there, Lucy," I say. "I'd love to read your books."

"Okay. They're about a character named Moo-moo. I hope you like that name?"

"I think it's an amazing name! Does he happen to be a cow?"

"Yes, sir."

Katrina lowers the puppet and looks at me. "Did you bring number seventy-nine?" she says.

I grab my notebook from the guest room and we collaborate on two more chapters of the saga of Moo-moo. By the time we're done, Moo-moo owns property in Las Vegas, which he's eager to turn into a cash cow. Get it? My mother calls the girls over to help make stuffing and I'm left with Ray, who can't stop yawning.

"You're making me tired," I tell him. "We haven't even gotten to the turkey and you've got me yawning."

"Rough, rough night last night."

"Party?"

"Everybody from high school is back. Thanksgiving. I must've done eleven shots with Greg Freedman and those cats. Rich kids with endless cash."

"So glad I missed it."

Ray faces me, a look of scorn.

"I know," I say. "I'm a pussy."

"Katrina has to go live with Lizzie's cousin in Atlanta."

I sit forward on the couch. "What'd you just say?"

"First of the month. I take her to Atlanta. Beats child services. Foster care."

"Dinner!" my wife says to the room.

"What are you talking about? Whose cousin?"

"Lizzie's. I know, I know. It sucks. You don't have to tell me."

"Ray?" I say.

"There's nothing I can do. Trust me, we've thought it out."

"You've thought it out. You've thought *what* out?"

"*Listen.* It's been hell with Lizzie. She's headed to rehab, man."

"Rehab? Lizzie's going to rehab? Why wouldn't you tell me this, Ray?"

I look behind me to see if Jackie or my mother can hear this. Ray is talking, using his hands for emphasis, but I'm not hearing him.

". . . the plan is to let her live with these second cousins. I don't know them."

"You don't know them? You don't know the cousins?"

"They're Lizzie's cousins," he says. "They're religious, but fine."

"Great. Great, Ray. What religion?"

"I don't know."

"Dinner," my mother says. "Come find your seat."

I picture Lizzie's relatives. Appalachian Mountains, missing fingers, inbreeding, men looking under the hood of a Chevy on cinderblocks. I stand and search the room for Katrina.

"You, Ray," I say, "have to be the father. Right? Aren't you capable of being her father?"

"What's that supposed to mean?" Ray says, flashing his famous rage. He looks like a constipated murderer, his head and neck quivering. "I can't take care of her."

"Why not?"

He stands and looks down at me. "I've got to travel to make money, pal."

"Since when?"

"Since I got an offer in Michigan to build houses."

I stare at him. "Build houses here."

"I have a connection there. The money is great. Someone's gotta make money."

"I don't believe what I'm hearing."

My brother and Anna saunter toward us, arm in arm. "Who are you?" Cam says to Ray.

"It's Ray, Cam. My friend Ray. You've met. A dozen times."

"I'm kidding, of course I know this guy. Aren't you the one who got busted for selling weed?"

Ray nods.

My brother puts his hand out. "How long they keep you in the clink for that?"

"Just two weeks," Ray says. "Then community service."

"This is my fiancée, Anna. Honey, this is my brother's friend. He's done time."

"It's so nice to make your acquaintance," Anna says and offers her hand.

"What do you do these days?" my brother asks.

Ray looks at me. "I'm a builder."

"Of what?"

"Homes."

Cam looks at me. He leaves it at that. Ray doesn't care. He's ogling Anna's tiny skirt.

"Dinner!" my mother says.

Cam and Anna move as one into the dining room. He points at a photograph of himself in college. She touches his face in the picture and then his real face. I don't feel so good. I ask Ray to come in the kitchen and he follows me.

"It's not my choice," he says.

"Why wouldn't it be your choice? You don't mean that."

"Lizzie's bipolar as shit. She needs medicine."

"Fine, Ray, get the medicine for her and fix it. You're the mother and father now. Do you see, it's yours to fix? Get on the job, man."

"It's not that fuckin' easy!"

"You made Katrina, right? She's not just gonna disappear because you're done with the task."

"No shit."

"She's not a fuckin' gerbil, right? You can't just stop loving the girl because you've gotta go."

"You're spitting on me, asshole," he says.

"Where's your mom, Ray? She's a grandmother, isn't she?"

He sort of skips at me, close to my face. "She's fucking drunk right now, man. It's six thirty on Thanksgiving and she's lit."

"We need you at the table," my mother says. "Please, guys. Turkey time!"

Ray walks toward the table. I can hardly move.

Cam is next to Alex. I'm next to Anna and my stepdad. I look at Katrina and envision her suitcase, the shipping off to Atlanta. I see my wife. She catches my eye and knows something's wrong. They're taking Katrina to a kennel. I sit heavily; my chair tips forward; a fork drops. Everyone looks at me.

"Sit much?" my brother says. Only Anna smiles.

I wipe my sweaty forehead with my napkin. I take three large gulps of red wine. My brother says he wants to make a toast.

"If you're doing gratefuls," my mother says, "you have to wait your turn. I promised someone special."

My brother's mouth is open, his wineglass held high. So unaccustomed to being told to wait.

"My granddaughter wants to be the first for grateful time."

Tara stands with a water glass in her hand. "I want to thank my mom and dad for loving me?"

Awwwww.

"I want to thank my mom for letting me quit choir?"

I face Katrina. Cherub skin, listening to Tara, her head tilted just so. I finish my wine and pour more.

"I want to thank my best friend Ginger for not telling Sarah Means that I thought she smelled like soup."

Katrina roars at this and looks at me. I smile back.

"And I want to say that I'm really glad my friend Katrina is here. And that I wish Kimmy was here. I miss her. PS, Katrina and I have the same sneakers. A coincidence."

Katrina removes one of her shoes and holds it high to the crowd.

My brother is awoken by the unexpected. "That's so thoughtful, Tara. I'm sure Kimmy misses you too."

Silence.

My mother looks upset, thinking of Kimmy. She needs to sit back in her seat and look out at all of us. She can't speak. My stepfather is up.

"I'm grateful for all of you," he says. "Just a whole lotta love to all of you. Happy Thanksgiving."

Light applause. My mother stands.

"Some Thanksgivings I've chosen to go around the table and talk about each of you. This year I'd like to single out just one person. I met this girl about twenty years ago. She was in love with my son. And now she's a woman. My daughter-in-law. Poise, beauty, smarts, sensitivity, an amazing mother of young children. And she works many hours a week in a company that must thank its lucky stars each morning that they have such a truly successful woman at the helm. Thank you for loving my son and grandchildren the way you do. And thank you for becoming like a daughter to me."

Applause. I watch my wife stand.

"Thank you. I love you too. Thank you for thinking of me, and for saying such sweet things. I'm grateful this year for all of you, each of my family members. Dad, I've never met a man like you. There is an integrity in you that cannot be matched. You and Mom made me the woman I am. You and Mom gave me the wherewithal to achieve on my own, which is so invaluable, something I promise to instill in my children. And with that said, you also raised me to be a kind person, able to cherish my family for who they are. Thank you. I hope you all have a wonderful year."

"I love you too, baby girl," her father says.

They blow kisses and she sits. Katrina's turn. Ray says something in her ear and she slowly stands.

"I'm grateful to Jay for writing stories with me. I read them at night sometimes and add to them," she says. "I want to be a writer someday." She sits with her notebook.

She gets a big round of applause. Ray tries to swallow a yawn. I ache for where Katrina is headed.

"Alex, your turn," my mother says.

"I think I'm gonna pass," he says, looking first at Anna.

"Not sure this year, babe?" Jackie says. "You can think about it."

"When I can't think of anything to be grateful for," my mother says, "I look around me and I see my sons, my grandchildren, my husband, my friends. And it's then I know how lucky I am. Lucky to be here, amongst people as wonderful as you are, Alex."

I feel tears behind my eyes, as if there's a warm syrup on the top of each eyeball. Five days on the new medicine. We've been warned it could get worse before it gets better. I've been watching his every move. He glances at Anna again and adjusts his silverware.

My father-in-law grips Alex's neck and kisses his head before he lifts half his body from the chair and says, "Love you all, thanks for the eats." He gets applause.

Ray stands.

"I want to thank you for inviting us. I actually hate this holiday. I think I said that last year too."

"You did, Ray," my mother says.

Laughter.

"Yeah, I remember. I'm grateful that I was able to look forward to coming here to eat with you all. I don't hate being a part of it this year. You make us feel like a family. We don't have anything close to this at our house. Right, Kat?"

She ignores the question. Ray puts his hands deep in his sweatshirt pockets and removes them. He faces his daughter.

"I'm sorry," he says to her. "I'm so sorry I don't have anything this nice at our house."

The quiet is terrible and I see my mother absorbing it. "That's why you need to come here each year. We'll always be here for you."

I try to touch Katrina's foot under the table. Our shoes bump and she looks up at me. I wave to her with my index finger. She does the same.

Cam stands, but keeps his hand in Anna's grip. He appears to be at a loss for words, his eyes flitting, glancing at the ceiling. "We met only because I was in pain."

Oh boy.

"It was, in fact, across the room and it was, in fact, in a bar, where they say you cannot, *cannot*, meet the person you'll spend the rest of your life with."

I watch my mother as she refolds her napkin with purpose.

"Where I've been, in the last many years . . . is a place that cannot be discussed in all circles. But I've had some loneliness," he says and drops his gaze to Anna. She looks unnerved, too smart to revel in the awkward spotlight. Cam sees no problem. "What word do people use when they want the world to know they've found a soul mate? What's a word stronger than *love*? Because I am *so* in love. I am so very much in love with you, Anna. You've saved my life."

The applause is wobbly. My mother is suddenly out of her chair and in the kitchen, bending over the stove. "Continue, please, I'll be there."

Besides me, this leaves my father-in-law's new girlfriend and Anna. *Seem*-ka takes a full ten minutes to tell a story about her mother and the first time she brined a Butterball in the bathtub. I notice Ray has his finger deep in his mouth, retrieving a piece of whatever, celery, cashew. The glimpse I get of his face makes me hate him in the moment. Too busy picking his teeth to care for his only child. Needs to send her away because he's so busy, just booked solid.

"So I guess I'm saying, thanks for having me."

I stand, applauding the brining story. "Hi. I'm grateful this year for my friend Katrina."

Ray looks up at me. And then Katrina does.

"I love my kids, and I really love my wife. Hi, honey."

"Hi."

"But this girl over here is very special to me. Did you know that the story Katrina and I have been writing for a while now has a brand-new chapter? So, if you're interested in reading it later, please see either me or Katrina."

Katrina holds the notebook up to the group. "See?" she says. "The story never ends. It just keeps going."

"And you're so fun to be with. I know exactly why your parents are so very proud of you!"

Ray's cell phone rings and he glances at the number before standing, his chair falling backward. "Yeah," he says. "It's me. What's up?" He walks into another room.

"Okay," my mom says, "did everyone go, did everyone have a turn?"

Anna stands. "I just want to say thank you. I know this hasn't been an easy year. Thank you for welcoming me into your home."

My mother nods to her with a smile. Cam kisses her as she sits.

"Let's eat," my stepdad says.

Ray is back in the room, his eyes intent, wide. He whispers into Katrina's ear and takes her by the hand. "I'm so sorry but we have to go," he says.

"What?" my mother says.

I stand as he pulls her a bit, knocking two clay turkeys onto the ground.

"What's going on, man?" I ask.

Ray shrugs. "My mother wants to see her and I told her we'd only be here for a bit."

"But she didn't eat yet," my mother says.

"It's okay," Ray says. "There's gonna be food at her house."

Katrina keeps her head down as Ray throws her coat on. He says good-bye by waving to the table and walks out on the porch. I follow them and put my hand on her shoulder.

"I was hoping you'd stay for dinner," I say. "I'm a little surprised you're just up and headed off like this. Katrina has a sock puppet in the kitchen. Can I grab it for you, Kat?"

She looks back at me. "Yes, please."

"We're already outside," Ray says. "I'll have to come back for it."

They walk to the driveway and he opens his truck door.

"Leave her with me," I say.

He moves forward, gets her seat belt on, and starts the engine. I walk to the car and he sees me. He rolls the window down.

"Leave her here with me. Leave her here with me."

He shuts the engine off, gets out of the truck, opens the passenger door, unhooks Katrina's seat belt, and walks her to me. He places her hand in mine and gets back in his truck without a word. Katrina and I watch Ray pull away, and down the street. We hear two dogs barking. Neither is my mom's. One has a deep, bellowing bark; the other sounds like a shih tzu trying to act tough.

"You hear that?" I ask her.

"No."

"The dogs."

"Oh. Yes, I do hear it," she says.

"There's a little one and a big one."

She says nothing.

"Let's go get some dinner, okay?"

She looks down the road, where she last saw her dad's car. She then sees me, tall above her, our hands clasped. We go inside and every eye is on us. So we sit back down at the table. And my wife pours her some juice.

🦙   🦙   🦙

I dream lightly. A farm. Cows, geese, and an okapi. The toilet is running in the hallway of my mom's house and I can hear it while still admiring the animals. I think I find peace in the word *farm*, the idea of it. An artist makes something of nothing, a harvest begins. I see the girls in the barn: my daughter, Katrina, Kimmy. They want to sit on the horses. One is white, the other spotted brown. Katrina has a carrot. She feeds it to the white horse. I hear tires on the driveway. It's not in the dream. Not a screech but the whine of turning tires on pavement. I'm awake. I run down the stairs and to the front door before he can knock. Ray is walking onto the porch.

"Hey, sorry it took so long," he says. He's been drinking for sure. His feet never stop shifting.

"Is she asleep?" he says.

"Of course, man."

"Unfortunately, I have to take her. You wouldn't believe how much crap I got from my mother for leaving her here on Thanksgiving night."

"It's okay," I say, searching for time. "But she's sound asleep."

"Yeah, but I gotta take her," he says and walks past me into the house.

I see my fight light. A flickering bulb of red inside my cranium. I fight only during perfect storms. Ray walks into my mother's house at 1:30 a.m as if it's noon.

"Which room is she in, bud?"

"No room," I say.

"What?"

"She's not in any room that you're going in right now."

His forehead scrunches as he approaches me. Intimidation 101.

"Where's my daughter sleeping?"

"She's in my mother's room, on the couch. You gonna walk in my mother's bedroom, Ray?"

"Why the hell would you put her in there?"

"Go home, Ray. Come back in the morning."

He is not happy. He begins to pace, but more like a rapper than an expectant father. I stand there, an AA therapist trying to wait out my patient's furious rhythm. He stops and faces me, allowing whatever drug he's on to override his inhibitions.

"Go get my daughter!"

"She's asleep," I say. "She's a little girl and she's asleep. Come back in the morning."

"No! I need her now. I'm not waking up at my mom's without her. Now go get her and stop being an asshole. She'll fall asleep in the car and I'll just carry her up to bed."

"I'm going back to sleep," I say. "You can crash here if you want to. She'll be right over there making sock puppets in the morning."

He walks up to me, his nose next to mine. We had a fight when we were sixteen, after he took a bottle of Crown Royal from his mother's liquor cabinet. We drank too much and ended up wrestling, then punching each other.

"I don't want to fight," he says. "I just want my kid."

We stare at each other for a moment and we both know what it means.

"Please stop," I say, and he tries to scoot by me. I open my arms and block him.

"Dude," he says, "get the fuck out of my way."

He gives me a shove and I have to backpedal to gain my balance. In my mind the choice to defend my mom's house is clear and well thought out. I take one step and with an open hand I blast his left cheek with a hardy snap of my palm. The contact leaves him holding his face and nearly spun around but on his feet. When he faces me his expression suggests shock and fury so when he darts at me I can only brace my legs and wait for impact. All his body weight is thrown onto me and we fall, crashing into the wall between the kitchen and living room. An earthquake of noise erupts and his chin is against mine before he grips my T-shirt to punch me in the face. His fist cocks back and he's gone, off of me, swung around by Cam, who has Ray's body bent backward over his own.

"Dad?!" Alex says, and I feel his hand on my elbow.

"You gonna hit my brother?" Cam says, more calmly than you'd think, choking Ray with locked fingers around his neck.

"Wait," I say and pull my arm from Alex. "Cam, enough. Stop!" Ray can't breathe. "Cam, enough!" I yell. He flips Ray off of him and pops to his feet like a wrestler. Ray is on his side, holding his neck in my mother's front hall, among the owl figurines and fading smell of pie. When I turn around my mother and stepfather are with Alex, squinting in the dark.

"What's happening?" my mother says.

"It's Ray," I say. "He's going to come back tomorrow."

My mother looks at Cam. He's out of breath, smiling, a scratch on his face.

"Please go back to bed," I say. "It's all fine."

They do, slowly, even Alex. I have no idea what he saw. I sit and glare at my old friend, waiting for him to leave.

"You fucked up," he says, standing. "You should've just gotten her for me. Stay out of my life, Jay. And go get my *fucking* little girl!"

"Not tonight."

He skips toward me again and Cam is too far away. His fist rears back to hit me. I zone out, the way bad drivers subconsciously accelerate into crashes. The punch lands high on my left cheek. It's worse than I thought. Powerful. I absorb the flash of white light, the immediate aching pang to my skull. I sit in a flop on the kitchen floor. I don't see or even hear Cam drag Ray to his truck. I only feel the arms of my son, falling lightly over me like a tarp from the cold. His hair I can smell, and it's sweet like sleep. His hands tighten around my arms and his back is a shield, curled and flexed, a wall from the pain. I move my cheek to his and taste a tear that is not mine.

"I'm sorry," he says.

"Sorry for what?"

"Jay?" my brother says.

I stand and Alex helps me.

"I don't think this idiot can drive," he says, and we all hear Ray start the truck. "Oh well, he's leaving after all."

"Good," Alex says.

"Is your dad hurt, Alex?"

He looks at me closely. "He got punched in the eye."

"You've *got* to make better friends than this guy," Cam says. "Why do you still hang out with this person?"

"It's so out of hand," I say.

We all hear the truck again, rolling up the street. Ray parks it with a screech.

"Dad?" Alex says and our hands clasp.

"He's all bark. It's always been the same."

Cam is in the front hall closet. He finds an umbrella and jogs onto the porch.

I walk Alex down the hallway. "He's not coming inside again. I promise. Let's go to sleep."

In the guest room, we sit face to face on his bed.

"It's swelling," he says, and our eyes connect. I kiss his head and lie down next to him. We hear Cam walk in and head to his room. I listen to Alex's breath, so careful, shallow, and think he might be listening for the truck. But it finally grows calm and metered, and I hold him, as the holiday ends.

Kidnap

Advil helps. But the throbbing rises as soon as it wears off. It feels like a swollen sunburn, wet with A&D, the only topical I could find. I dream about the farm again. This time I have bigger horses and Alex is along. My daughter and Katrina are holding heads of lettuce. The horses chomp and eat quicker than they would in real life. The most aggressive stallion bites down and gets a piece of Alex's hand. He hollers, gripping it, dancing in circles. I try to comfort him but there's blood. Through his fingers it falls and I reach to catch it. It's all over me. I'm awake at 6:00 a.m. Just a dream. My beautiful son's arm is draped over my chest.

A close look in the bathroom mirror shows an abrasion, just at the tip of the swelling. Ray won't remember any of it. I hear my mother making breakfast for the girls. Eggs, sock puppets, bacon, the TV on CNN, too loud. I blink and gaze again at my shiner. I am impotent. But still a fighter. My wife walks in the hallway bathroom and lifts her toothbrush.

"What the hell happened to your face?"

I get an ice baggie and a kiss and her hand rubbing my back. I tell the story about Ray and Cam at 1:30 a.m. We hide my face from the girls as long as possible and then explain that I slipped but I'm fine, no worries. My brother tries to touch the puffed area, his finger stupid, robust. "He really got ya," he says.

"Thanks," I say to him. "Thanks for helping me. I had my hands full."

He tries to touch the bruise again and I dodge him.

"What are brothers for?"

I like that he says this. I try to tell him without words.

"Well, we're off to New York," Cam says, checking his watch and eyeing the stairs for Anna.

My mother, still in her robe, approaches him and kisses his cheek. "Where you two headed?" she asks, allowing the new day to be just that.

"Anna's never been to Manhattan," he says. "So, kid in a candy store." He grins and rubs his gloved hands together.

My mother's smile is warm, forgiving. "You like her."

He nods quickly, a boy with an ice cream cone. "I do."

"I'm happy for you, Cam."

"Thanks, Ma."

"But your lack of empathy for how I might be feeling about my granddaughter, not to mention my daughter-in-law is bordering on criminal."

All the color leaves his face.

"If you go to your apartment," my mother says, "I want you to collect every photograph of Kimmy that you can find and . . ."

"Good morning," Anna says on the stairs.

"Good morning," I say.

"Good morning, Anna," my mother says.

"Okay, Ma," Cam says. "It's a plan. I'll do just that."

"Thank you," she says and gives Anna a quick hug.

Cam steers her by her shoulders through the front door. Anna turns to me as she passes. "Wait, what happened to your face?"

"I'll tell you all about it," Cam says.

When the door closes, my mother walks away, into her bedroom. I'm not sure if I should follow her. The girls are playing. The TV is blaring. No call from Ray. I sit on the couch with a bag of frozen peas on my face. The clock moves slowly, the agenda so open, a Friday. I see my mother. I cannot tell if she's been crying. She asks if I have Kimmy's cell number. I do; we try it.

"Hi, busy saving the planet, you know what to do after the beep. If this is you, Lindsay, you left your Furby here and it's vibrating. I think it's hungry. Weird, I smell toast." *Beep.*

"I think she may have lost her phone," I say.

1:00 p.m. 2:00 p.m. 3:00 p.m and there's no call from either Ray or Lizzie. I begin to play a game in my head. It involves Katrina and Florida. I take her for a week. But I keep her as my own. We skip Atlanta and just move on, as if she's ours. I see the girls and Alex outside with my mom and wife. Sidewalk chalking and then flower cutting. I walk to them, listen to the patter.

"We need to cut the stem down here. See that?" my wife says. "This way the flower will grow and grow again. You don't want to cut it too low, or too young."

My mother and my son sit with me on the front porch. Alex stares at my bruise. He touches his own eye. I reach for his knee and he doesn't shoo me away.

"Did Ray call?" my mother asks.

I shake my head, look at my watch. No call. No text.

"If I had the balls, I'd take her to Florida. Raise her as my own."

When I glance at my mother she's looking at me. "People raise other people's children all the time. I see it in my practice constantly. It's usually the grandma. You have to hold the cubes directly on the bump, sweetie."

"It's legal, to just take someone's child?"

"No, you can't just take her, of course not. Here," she says, and centers the baggie.

"Ow."

"I know."

"What if it's dire?" I ask. "What if she's being neglected under my nose? What do people do?"

"You have to involve the authorities," she says. "There'd need to be a specific reason for the investigation. Child services would . . ."

"Neglect," I say.

"Children are better off with their mothers. If they can't have their mom, then Dad is best."

"Have you met Lizzie?"

"Of course. She's like a billion other girls. Got pregnant and isn't prepared for the job."

"They want to ship her off. To Atlanta."

My wife and daughter pile clippings on Katrina's outstretched arms.

"What if he doesn't come?" I say. "What if it's Saturday and they haven't called?"

My mother faces me. "They're coming for her. Trust me. They are coming for their girl."

※　　※　　※

Ray shows up at 8:00 p.m. I jump from the couch, half crushed, half relieved. My mother stands with me. "He's here. Katrina!"

I wait in the doorway, see him in the driveway. And then I don't. I step off the porch and he's squatting in the street. And spitting. "Ray?"

I startle him. His gaze is blurred, his eyes bloodshot.

"Did Lizzie come to get Kat?" he asks.

"No."

"Did you call Lizzie?" he asks.

"No, Ray. That wasn't the plan. I don't even have her number."

"Good, good," he says. "Get Katrina. I have to take her home now. I'll wait here."

I know he doesn't remember last night. I touch my face and look back at the house. My mother and wife are on the porch.

"Ray, I was thinking. Maybe you need to sleep a bit more."

"I have responsibilities," he says, trying to find my eyes.

"I can't believe you're so fucked up, man."

"I'm not fucked up."

"I'm not sure you want to drive with Katrina."

He lets this thought germinate, his chin lowering. He looks at his car. His watch. He sits down on the driveway. "Call Lizzie," he says. "She'll come get her."

"You call Lizzie, Ray. Tell her to call me."

"Fine," he says and reaches for his phone. As he dials, he stands and gets back in his car. He doesn't drive away.

"Ray?"

He starts the engine and leaves.

I sit in my mother's living room with Katrina, my daughter, my son, my stepfather, and my wife. Katrina yawns and I watch her head lean against Jackie's shoulder.

My phone rings. It's Lizzie. I walk into the kitchen and Jackie follows me. "I have Katrina here, Lizzie."

"Yeah, I know. I don't know why he left her there," she says. "Anyways, I can't come get her till I get my boyfriend's truck back. He should be back from Nutley in about an hour but I can't be sure."

"Okay."

"Can you keep her for one more night?"

"Lizzie?"

"Yeah?"

"I was wondering if you'd be okay if we took Katrina to Florida for a week . . . or so."

"Florida?"

"Yeah, the girls are getting along like sisters, and we thought, let's give her a week down there, while you and Ray talk things out."

"You payin'?"

"Of course."

"You better ask Ray."

"I will."

"She's supposed to be heading to Atlanta on the fifth."

"Yes, I heard about Atlanta. Things must be pretty rough for you, huh?"

My wife is staring at me.

"I don't know," Lizzie says in a wobbly voice. She is silent.

"You there, Liz?" I ask.

"Take her for now. I'll call Ray. Thanks." She hangs up.

I walk back to the family. I look at my wife, my mother.

"Hey?" I say, and stick my hand out to Katrina for a thumb-wrestling match. She smiles and grabs my hand. "One, two, three, four, let's have a thumb war." Our thumbs bump and hers lands on top.

"One, two, three," she says. "But you let me win."

"I was wondering if you'd like to come to Florida with us for a week. Or so."

My daughter jumps in the air. "Really?"

Katrina takes it all in, our hands releasing from the war.

"What about my school?" she says.

"Only a week," my wife says. "We'll get you right back to school after you visit."

"What did my dad say?"

My wife plays with her ponytail. "Well, your mom said yes and now we just have to ask your dad."

Katrina gives in to the excitement and jumps up and down with my daughter. "We're going on a plane together, we're going on a plane together."

My mother walks to me. "Call it a vacation," she says. "For now, it's just a vacation."

December 1

Teri scares me. She knocks on my passenger window in a cheerleader outfit. Two other women wait for her on the sidewalk, both in matching collegiate uniforms. "Did you get my calls?" she says.

"I was in New Jersey. You're a cheerleader."

"Handing out flyers for Sports Day next week. You're coming, right?"

"Oh, well, maybe."

"What happened to your eye?"

"I slipped. Look who I have," I say, glancing behind me.

"Who's this young lady?" she asks.

Katrina sits alone in the back seat. We have an appointment in ten minutes to see if I can enroll her this late in the school year. I think of how to explain it all and stumble to start. "She's the daughter of a friend. She's staying with us right now. This is Teri, Katrina. She's Ginger's mom."

"Hi."

"Hi, Katrina, such a gorgeous name. I wish I'd reached you both now. We had a bonfire on the beach last night. Cam and Anna hosted. I tried to call you."

Cam had a party and didn't invite us. We haven't spoken since he swooped in, saved us a lot more noise. Ray could've killed me. Perhaps Cam sees it as his final act of brotherly love. What more can he give? My mother says he's ignoring her too, that she knew confronting him might leave him "elusive" for awhile. I see Katrina's reflection in Teri's sunglasses. She's reading her notebook and laughing to herself, her hand over her mouth.

"Ginger wants to have friends to the house on Friday night," Teri says. "You should come, bring the kids, Katrina. I'll cook. You can do some writing on the deck if you'd like. It'll be private, quiet. Come anytime this week." Teri's hand is up for a high five. "Sound good?"

"I'll check with my wife," I say and fist-bump her open palm.

She sniffs, stands straight from leaning on the car. "I'd love to meet her again."

"I'm sure she feels the same."

Teri waves to Katrina, stepping back toward her friends. "Hope to see you soon. If not sooner."

🦋   🦋   🦋

The school meeting goes well. The only problem is I'm not her father, mother, or legal guardian. So we need permission from Ray or Lizzie. I call him and get his voice mail. He does not call me back. My wife and I are at the school the next day. She makes a pitch to the vice principal to let Katrina start at half tuition for the last six months of the school year with the stipulation that she may need to return to New Jersey at any moment.

"We'll eat the cost," she says.

The school agrees. The next two days are spent buying the school uniform, getting her medical paperwork, and going back and forth from Teri's mansion on the beach. The woman was right about the amazing writing spot. I open #79 and start freewriting about the day. It's warm, even tropical, but with spurts of flavored breezes. The scent in the air has color. My wife arrives straight from a convention in Chicago. She finds me alone on the deck. I introduce her to Teri, explaining just how generous she's been with Tara. They recall meeting at the river a while back. From the deck I see Katrina wearing her new purple bathing suit and a Tampa Bay Rays baseball cap. My daughter and Ginger stand next to her. The girls run up to join us and my wife squirts lotion on them. They jump in the pool like twins. Jackie and I walk down to the sand, hand in hand. We stroll in and out of the surf.

"I'm going to New York tomorrow," she says. "I think I'll be assigned a new title."

"Like what?"

"I don't know. Or care. Thinking about what's next, though; you should probably do the same."

I hear her. I see her. The words can only mean we will leave. I think of Alex, another transition. All while his body absorbs the medication. I think of Katrina.

"California," Jackie says. "I think we should go back. I think we should move our life back there."

We stop along the water's edge. I bury my feet in the sand and wait for them to disappear. We agree to keep the news quiet for now, and join the rest of the crew by the pool. Tara, Katrina, and Ginger play on a raft in the deep end. Teri's made lunch. I look out at the ocean. I will miss these views, the endless space. When the school year ends, we'll leave forever.

⛤   ⛤   ⛤

In the morning Jackie is off to New York. I can get access to Katrina's medical paperwork only if either of her parents gives consent on the phone. I try Ray's cell again and leave another message.

"I need you to call me back. I need to know if it's okay if I enroll Katrina in school here. She also needs permission from you to get a medical exam. Please call me back."

After school Tara and Katrina want to go to Teri and Ginger's house again. We arrive at the beach about 4:00 p.m. and Katrina and I write three full chapters in #79. Moo-moo is not only going to law school at Harvard but also has a girlfriend, a sheep named Phyllis. When we finish, I write alone, on the deck, the sky and water in my reach. My pen, an open page. By the end of the afternoon I've finished a story about a guy who writes a best-selling children's book with his friend's little daughter. They write in tandem about an amazing cow named Moo-moo. I put the characters in an apartment in Elizabeth, New Jersey, and specify that Moo-moo has emancipation papers: by law, he can never be eaten.

The sky is turning dark now, time to go. Katrina and my daughter are wrapped in towels in the back seat. As I turn onto our block I see our new neighbors directly across the street. Dad, Mom, and two daughters. I feel responsible to tell them about the flooding, the sandbags, the kayaks. No one moving onto this street knows what they're in for. The whole block is below sea level. I park the car, the girls pour out, and I see Alex sitting alone on the porch in a rocking chair. He is gazing out at the new family, perhaps at the older girl. I have not seen him out of the house since we returned from Thanksgiving. I play with the idea that the medicine is working. A muddy windshield wiped clean, as the doctor described the relief he should receive. I sit in the chair next to his and attempt words that will not launch him from the moment.

"They look nice. The new family."

Out of the corner of my eye I see him nod.

"I think I'll go over and warn them about the rain, the flooding. Do you want to come with me?"

I watch him consider it. He looks again; the older girl is very pretty.

Tara and Katrina run up the front walkway.

"We want to make them cookies, Daddy. The new neighbors. We'll make chocolate chip and sugar cookies for them."

"Okay, okay. You make the cookies and we'll bring them over."

My son is up from the chair, catapulted back in the house.

"Alex, wait."

Too late.

My phone rings. It's Ray.

"Put her on a plane," he says.

"Hi, there," I say. "Hold, please. Girls, I need to take this call. I'll meet you inside."

They walk back down the walkway. I see Tara waving to the new family.

"I've been calling you, Ray."

"Put her on a plane tonight. *Tonight!* Tell me what time to pick her up in Newark."

"Listen first. Okay? I haven't heard from you since Thanks-giving."

"Put my kid on a plane tonight or I'm calling the cops and sending a fucking Black Hawk helicopter to hunt you down."

"Oh, oh, really? Seems a little harsh, man. We're on our way to buy cookie batter."

"How 'bout I come to *fuckin'* Florida!" he barks. "Pick up your daughter and fly her back here. How do you think you'll sleep, *asshole?*"

"I got permission from your wife, Ray!"

"She's not my wife!"

"From Lizzie."

"Listen you motherfucker. We are finished as friends. I'm gonna come down there and stab your ass if you don't put her on a plane. *Tonight. Now!*"

I hang up. My heart is beating through my neck. I squeeze the arms of the rocking chair and envision Katrina in the hands of Ray. Lizzie. I call my wife. I get her voice mail.

"We have a problem," I say. "Call me."

My phone rings. It's Ray again. I let it ring.

"Yes, Ray."

"You're *wanted*, motherfucker. You kidnapped my daughter and I'm coming after your ass. Do you hear me? Do you fuckin' hear me?"

"She's too important."

"What'd you say?"

"She's too important to leave with you. Come get me, Ray. Come down here with your helicopter and try to pull your daugh-ter out of school. Gas her up, pal. I'll be waiting." *Click.*

"Daddy?" says Tara.

"What?"

"We don't have any cookie batter."

"We'll have to get some."

"Daddy?"

"Yes?"

"Katrina can turn her tongue all the way around. Do it, Kat. Do the three sixty."

Katrina's tongue is out, trying to flip over. My daughter laughs. "OMG. How do you do that?"

"You guys ready to get cookie batter?"

"Yes."

"Yes."

I stand and head back to the car. I call my wife again and get her voice mail.

"Please call me as soon as you get this," I whisper into the phone. "Ray called. He's making threats."

I pull out of the driveway.

"Jay?" says Katrina

"Yes?"

"Can I call my mom?"

I turn my body to see her. "Of course. Of course you can, Kat. I'll dial her number right now."

"Thanks. I want her to know how much I like it here."

Strapped in her seat belt, Tara leans over to hug her. "We love you too," she says.

I dial Lizzie and hand Katrina my phone. She gets voice mail.

"Hi Mom. It's Katrina. You can call me on this number. I've seen dolphins like three times. Real dolphins. In the water, right next to me almost. Hope you're happy. Bye."

She hands me the phone. And we head off for cookies.

Family Dinner

THURSDAY | *The wind has two skinny palm trees wrestling like giraffes*

I light the grill and find myself glancing at passing helicopters. The notion that Ray could procure such a machine is laughable. But even funnier is my searching for him in the skies over St. Petersburg. I sit across from Alex and have Katrina and Tara at my side. The asparagus is right, not too soft and just enough oil and pepper. It comes down to timing and Tara hates it when it's mushy. Grilling it indirectly is the key. The pork tenderloin and rice pilaf are a hit with Katrina. She eats while Tara talks.

"We could also make them brownies. Or a cake. If we make a cake we can write 'Welcome to the neighborhood' on it."

"Cookies are the best," Katrina says. "And we already bought the batter."

I look up at Alex. He's eating slowly, the earbuds in.

"What do you think, buddy?" I say.

He doesn't hear me. Tara touches his elbow and Alex reluctantly removes one earbud. "What?"

"Dad has a question for you."

"What kind of dessert should the girls make for our new neighbors?"

"I don't know," he says and plugs his ear again.

Katrina takes a long sip of her juice and rests the glass on the table. "Maybe we can do a little research. We can ask them what they like. But in a secret way."

"If you ask them," says Tara, "they're going to know we're baking them something and the surprise is over."

"I know," Katrina says, "but if you surprise them with a chocolate cake and one of them's allergic, then the surprise is like, 'Surprise! You need medicine now.'"

"I say we do a vanilla cake with chocolate frosting and write 'Welcome to the neighborhood' on it."

"Then we bought the wrong thing," I say. "We only got chocolate chip cookies."

"We'll need to go back," Tara says, her fork held above her head. "Tonight!"

"Not tonight," I say. "Tomorrow. Today is over. Anyone want more pork, rice, asparagus?"

"Yes, please," says Katrina.

I give her more and put the plate in front of her.

"You're a really good eater," Tara says.

"I like this food a lot," says Katrina.

"I think a dozen cookies is better than one cake," says Alex.

I look at him. His eyes are on Tara and Katrina. The headphones are out of his ears. Tara is staring at him, the way you'd look at your dog if he asked for directions. Alex stands, brings his plate to the sink, and leaves the kitchen. Tara and I have a moment, a smile. Who was that boy, who spoke to us at the dinner table?

"A dozen chocolate chip cookies it is," says Tara.

Come Home

FRIDAY | *They say a storm is coming*

Teri calls and says there are dozens of dolphins in the bay and we must gather our stuff and join her for the afternoon. We head over there after school, not realizing she's invited half the town for a party. From the driveway I can't be recognized with all the gear blocking my face. Umbrellas, towels, shovels, and chairs. We fall down on the beach, and I look up at my writing spot, nearly as high as the palm trees that shade it. Some guy is sitting there and Teri is putting lotion on his shoulders. I'm not jealous; it's just my writing spot and he's there, with Teri, not writing, so, it's not jealousy. Because I'm happily married.

When I get back up to the deck I see Tara, Katrina, and Ginger walking into the den with all their American Girl doll equipment. There's a stagecoach and a dune buggy, not to mention eighty pairs of tiny socks. More and more school folks arrive. The painter, my long-haired pal, comes with a skinny Asian woman named Chihiro. He introduces her as his English student and they both giggle at the absurdity. Herb is alone, holding a box of Glenlivet like a baby in his arms. We all see dolphins, just off the shore, a pod, maybe twelve. What a gorgeous day. My daughter and Katrina run from the den with handfuls of broccoli and carrots. Is it me or does Katrina look healthier, her skin, even the shine of her reddish hair? I'll use these empowered seconds to separate Ray from my mind, as if filing him away for the afternoon. I think of Alex. I take a deep breath and lift my arms high over my head into a stretch. Perhaps it's my responsibility to put myself in positive situations in which water meets horizon and the dorsal fins of wild dolphins appear. Inspired beyond reason I remove #79 from my bag and write the word *joy*.

Splash!

Ginger's mom and another bikinied woman jump in the pool. My phone rings. It's my wife.

"Sounds like a party," she says.

"Not really. How's the trip been going?"

A woman in a red bikini and heels hands me a beer. Her top lip is much fatter than her bottom one. "You looked thirsty," she says and grins through the Botox.

"Kosher for now," my wife says. "I'll be home tonight. Taking the last flight."

"Great."

"Did Ray call again?"

"No. No helicopters either."

"What about Lizzie?"

"No answer. We're just relaxing out here. I wish you were here."

"Is Katrina okay?"

I look at her in the pool with her neon goggles and flippers, trying to pull off three full flips underwater.

"Maybe we should just . . . get her back to her parents," Jackie says. "I don't know. I'm getting a little scared."

"Let's just see how the next week unfolds," I say. "Let's just see."

We hang up and I see him, my brother, Cam. He opens his arms to embrace me. Katrina runs over, dripping from the pool, to whisper something in my ear. "I lost my towel."

"Just grab another from the bin over there," I say.

Cam sits on the edge of my chair and removes his sunglasses. "That's Ray's kid."

I look at Katrina. My brother awaits an explanation. "Mom's looking for you," I say.

"Oh, yeah?"

"She's upset you left New Jersey without saying good-bye."

"I got enough problems."

"How about your daughter?" I ask. "Have you spoken to Kimmy?"

His face tightens, as if he's thinking: Why would you bring up my daughter's name here? Why would you greet me with the most painful issue in my life? Who do you think you are? By my elbow he pulls me out of earshot of everyone. "Are you Father Christmas?" he asks.

"I don't know what that means."

"Keep your thoughts about my divorce to yourself. For now, I need to leave the past behind. If this makes you uneasy, then too fuckin' bad for you. I don't owe you or my mother a *thing*. Do not mention Kimmy's name again. All day. Got it?"

He walks away.

Teri and Ginger start a volleyball tournament in the pool. Cam is the star, of course, slamming the ball over the net as if competing for cash. Tara and Katrina are on the same team but Ginger is on Cam's team. I watch, root for the girls, wish my son wanted to be here. When they finish the game we eat fish and chips and drink more beers. A guy named Chipper arrives with some of his friends. They're all just back from golf and the stories they tell include words like *back nine, sandpit, seven iron, slice, bogie,* and *Titleist.* The chemistry of the party changes instantly. The cool kids are here, and they're all wearing checkered slacks. Chipper is a large presence, and wants to know if I play. I say, "All the time," and he doesn't hear the sarcasm. He wants to know what club I belong to. "I don't play," I admit. He shows me his swing, his footing, his balance. His breath reeks of whisky and cigars. What a dreamboat.

"Daddy, I need a towel," my daughter says from the pool. I approach her and hand her one. *Splash!* Chipper has chosen to push me into the pool. Under water briefly, I ponder this move, especially the fact that it came from some golf dick I just met.

When I emerge, Cam is cackling his ass off with apologetic eyes. "Oh, you got punked, pal!" my brother says.

"Sorry, you were just so close," Chipper says.

I climb out, still holding my Red Stripe. It has pool water in it now. My daughter stares at me, her eyes tense, awaiting my reaction. I had no shirt on; my bathing suit was already wet. It was funny. I sit back down with the group, trying to dilute the obvious bully-to-nerd ratio by sipping from the drink I went in with. My ease with it all gets me some empathy from Teri. Cam is still snickering. He grips my shoulder as if massaging away my embarrassment, but pinches the muscle instead. When Chipper wants a fist bump I ignore him.

"Go fuck yourself" is what comes out of my mouth. Only the two transplants from New Jersey clap for this. The silence is too long. Teri ends it with a memory of last year's Halloween party, when Chipper got pushed in the pool in his *Dog the Bounty Hunter* costume.

The weirdness fades, I'm fine, no biggie. But my pinkie toe feels weird. When I went in the pool my feet were stunned and tried to keep planted. My small toe was the last to let go. I walk inside and into the bathroom. It's bleeding and purple, the nail torn. It's only when my brain connects with the sight that the toe begins to throb. Great. I come out and Teri is there. She sees the injury and tells me to go upstairs into her bathroom for Band-Aids and Neosporin.

"Chipper's been an asshole since high school," she says.

I walk up her regal staircase. Photographs of the family run along the wall. I look for hubby but see no men his age. I look for Teri and see her. In the photo she's a brunette with a Dorothy Hamill haircut, a different human being, waving at the Disneyworld entrance. I find myself in her bathroom. It is huge, like a normal person's bedroom. It has enormous closets that run off into other rooms. I hear her behind me and look back and see her by the doorway. Why she'd be up here with me I don't know. Maybe she's come to seduce me. I'd have to write to *Penthouse Forum*. My daughter's friend's mother.

And then I see her. Her body, nude, as she wraps a white towel around herself. I see her again, a glimpse, but it's just her reflection in the mirror. I find the Band-Aids.

"Chipper's been married three times," she says.

I look again but cannot see her.

"Wives two and three were both friends of mine. Sahara, the second, was also married to my ex and they had a daughter named Emily, who is my goddaughter. So, I despise the man but I have to deal with him because I'm related to him in a weird way. I brought you a beer."

She appears from one of the closets, in only a towel. "Your toe looks bad," she says, worried. "I'm so sorry that happened, Jay. Here's the beer."

She hands it to me. I take it from her hand and her towel falls to the floor. In the seconds our eyes meet, my brain floods with regressive memories that leave my gut burning. Her body is there, in the presence of me, a married man, a monarch of monogamy. I see my wife, glimpses of our wedding, still shots, the cake, her dress, her father making a speech. Teri steps toward me. I don't look away; I don't walk away; I don't come through and simply say, "No!" Instead I stand there, allowing the crime of it to breach the moat I've been digging for so long. Frozen, I await the slinking woman whose breasts dangle as she moves like an Internet porno come to life. All I can feel is my penis filling with blood like a water balloon connected to a fire hose. I'm a villain, an ape who's been shoved to the precipice of raw, human error. And I'm too far gone to survive as I was before. The danger will thrash me, ruin me, nullify my intentions with a fluid slashing of my windpipe. Her head, the top of her head, comes at me. Other than my wife's, I haven't seen an adult's head so close to me in over two decades. She drops to the floor and separates my knees.

"Teri?"

She stands and kisses me on my lips. "I really like you."

It's the first sexual kiss I've had in twenty years that didn't come from my wife.

"Don't help me be a bad person."

"You're a good person," she says.

I limp out of the bathroom with a broken toe and my first erection in days. I cover it with my T-shirt.

"I have to go home."

I find my daughter and Katrina all the way in another wing of the house. Katrina is placing American Girl doll slippers onto wide plastic feet.

"We're outta here, let's go."

"Why?"

"Mom's on her way."

"We want to stay," says Tara.

I lift her from the floor by her armpits.

"Hey, I'm not a doll, ya know."

"I forgot about a thing I have to do. And Mom is flying home. I'm sorry."

On my way to collect the chairs and towels I see Teri. She is wearing a robe.

"Can I talk to you?" she says.

I shake my head. "I have to go," I say.

"I'm sorry," she says, her face softening.

"Teri. I didn't mean for that to happen."

"Me neither," she says.

I convince myself it's nothing. But only in bursts. Guilt. It hovers, questions, awaits the weak, and settles in like termites. I had a bad toe, I went up to the bathroom, I had to find a Band-Aid. I gave in to possibility. I am a man. Not a housewife. I come from Mars. I'd take that woman and ravish her if I were single. But I did not ask her to place me among the hunted. I was just sitting there. I pushed Chipper's buttons, perhaps, which led him to push me in the pool. This woman, my friend, became nude in a snap. Am I guilty? Did I break the code?

"Daddy?"

"Yes, baby?"

"You're driving very fast."

It begins to rain. The buildup is quick. My eyes jump to the rearview mirror. I see my daughter, staring back at me in the back seat, her forehead pinched like mine. I smile, trying to get her to do the same.

"Wanna sing? *When I was a little bitty boy, just up off the flooooor,*" I sing.

"Twenty questions," Tara says.

"Okay, I'm thinking of an animal," I say.

"Is it a mammal?" my daughter says.

"Yes."

"Is it a dolphin?" Katrina says.

I find her in the rearview. "You're really good at this."

"Katrina, you're a genius."

I pull onto our street and we see our new neighbors. I suggest the girls go meet them but it's pouring rain now.

"But we didn't make the cookies yet," says Tara.

Alex is in the den, watching TV. A weatherman is pointing at a computer screen. "It's name is Wilma," he says, "and she's bordering between a tropical storm and an actual hurricane. It should either veer from us or hit us directly by sunrise."

"A storm," I say, and Alex nods.

"Is Mom in the air?" he says.

"Should've landed by now."

He looks at me. "How do you know?"

"Daddy?" Tara yells.

"Yeah?"

"Where's the cookie batter?"

I find the batter in the fridge and Katrina butters the cookie sheet.

An hour later my wife walks in and Tara and Katrina race to her, attack her, open the gifts, smell the world on her overcoat. She is beautiful and loyal. I am not. Alex walks out of the den. This time he's standing next to his mother, waiting for her to hug him. She stands to embrace him and his head lowers onto her shoulder. Jackie's eyes close and she holds her son. "I'm glad you landed safely," he says and walks away. Jackie watches this kind stranger as he leaves the room.

"Was that our boy?"

I nod. "He ate with us. He was watching the weather and he sat on the porch, watching the new neighbors move in."

"Yes," she says. "Tell me all of it."

"I think I broke my toe," I admit.

We head to the living room where we bundle like penguins after a thousand-mile walk in the tundra. My wife asks how it happened and I shrug it off.

"Tell us about your trip," I say.

"Every step I took I thought of you guys. It was so long and busy. I just wanted to get back to my babies. Come here Katrina, you too, I want kisses."

"Don't leave anymore, Mama," my daughter says.

"I've been so lonely. I just want to be home with my puppies." I watch her kiss her little girl's shoulder, forehead, and wrists and the guilt bores a hole somewhere low in my bowel.

"Tara, you grew over the week," she says.

"I know. I can feel it in my shoes."

We soon grow calmer, sleepy in the warmth of each other. I watch my wife's eyes close, her torso leaning, her head on her daughter's hip. We all head to bed, and she is asleep in seconds. My thumb and pointer finger form a circle around her thin right wrist. Her breath falls into a sleepy rhythm and I listen to it, trying to be consoled by it. When she jolts awake she looks lost, maybe expecting the walls of a hotel, an empty space beside her. "Jesus," she says. "Where am I?"

The rain pummels the roof without letup.

"You're home."

"Need to take my contacts out." She's up and in the bathroom.

It's like I have a bump in my chest, my sternum. I touch it and it's raised.

She returns, falling onto the mattress. "I'm run too thin," she says. "I want to see my kids, be like other moms."

"I'm sorry."

"I want a third baby," she says.

I sit up and look down at the side of her face. The ceiling fan above us clicks just slightly. *Tck, tck, tck, tck, tck.*

"I have an appointment for a vasectomy," I say.

"Cancel it."

I think of Teri, the smell of her suntanned skin, her nude bikini line.

"I don't know."

"Let's just try."

"The last time we tried I was a no show, remember?"

"Give me a break."

"And then I went to Teri's house and ended up in that…mess."

"Ended up *what?*" she says.

Tck, tck, tck, tck, tck, tck.

"Ended up what, Jay?"

"I was in her bathroom. And Teri walked in without any clothes on."

Tck, tck, tck, tck, tck.

"Nothing happened," I say.

I hear rustling. "What did you do?"

"I did nothing."

"Did you kiss her?"

"No."

She swallows heavily. "Did you kiss her?"

"No. She kissed me."

She turns the light on. Her face shows the impact, her chin wrinkling, shoulders drooped.

"Nothing happened. Relax."

"Why did she kiss you?"

"I don't know."

"You gave her the impression it was all right to kiss you."

"No, no, not even close," I say.

"Why were you there? Tell me the story."

A broken toe? You must've coaxed her. You flirted first, used your eyes to invite her upstairs. Liar, betrayer, typical male. Loser, horndog, gorilla. You're a fool, a statistic in a world of lame, selfish animals. Everything you're saying is a lie. Don't you think men hit on me?

"I did not do anything! She kissed me. I did not kiss her."

"And that's the fucking problem, asshole! You should never have been there!"

She can see the entire scenario in her head, and it's the only visual she'll accept. I drank too much and reacted to the woman's advances too slowly. My wife's wary of me cheating and now it's all realized, the truth of every nightmare she's ever conjured. Like shrapnel it riddles our bed to shreds, empties all turrets.

"You want to be with that bimbo? Do you?"

Why do I shrink and not defend myself with energy? Because to defend too much can be construed as admission so I laugh to save the dignity I deserve. But she's reading my confusion as callousness. She's out of bed now and pacing. Naked, stumbling, ready to murder me, maybe, a Shakespearean stabbing. She ends up sitting on the floor, in tears, her nose running, her face pained, betrayed, undone. I sit next to her on the floor. I decide silence is best. But my mind is reeling: Aside from being innocent, and loving you more than anyone I've ever met, I wish you were here, wife. And I know you wish you were here too. I don't wish I were there, but it's only fair that I attempt to be there, so you can be here. Because if I were out there, you'd be here. Your here is there and my here is here. There's a knock on our bedroom door. My wife hops up and runs into the bathroom. I say come in and see Katrina, weeping, her new bathrobe in her grip. "I had a nightmare," she says.

I walk with her to our bed and lay her down in my spot. With her small face pressed into my pillow, she blinks her eyes and they search to close. "Do you want to talk about it?" I ask.

"No."

I turn the light out and find my wife at the sink. "It's Katrina. She had a bad dream."

She sees me in the mirror.

"I only love you," I say.

She nods angrily, walking past me. She gets in bed next to Katrina and pulls the blanket up to her ear.

"I had a nightmare," Katrina whispers.

My wife rubs her small back. "I know, sweetie. I'm so sorry. Let's have good dreams now. Only good dreams."

I'll sleep in Tara's room. Katrina's bed has been ordered but won't arrive for a week. The air mattress next to my daughter's bed is blown up like a trampoline. I try to get centered but feel as if I'm slowly drifting right. When I turn it squeaks like I'm sitting on a beach ball. My daughter sits up, stares at me, and falls back asleep. It's as if I did cheat on my wife. Exiled. It's easier to be the one who travels. Right? The stimulus for the leaver is new, even stunning, the air a bit more crisp. No, being home is easier. No long lines, no airport, no taxi, your very own bed. You call me and I say I miss you and you say you miss me and the kids agree, life is better with two parents. You tell me that your work colleague told your boss he thinks you're too garrulous in situations where conciseness would suffice. You hear this destructive/constructive comment through gossip from another peer, a person who seems to grow younger and more virile when tainting the corporate chemistry in question. If he weren't a handsome gay man, he'd be a Jewish grandmother from Livingston, New Jersey, known as "the mixer." This small but heady piece of news gets stacked on your brain and I can envision you rubbing the shit out of your exhausted eyes and grinding your mental gears to figure out how to be perfect under such scrutiny. And how to save us, your family, from going hungry, sleeping under a torn tarp in a public playground. I think I'm going to write a novel. That's the job I want. A story about human connectivity, the crucial aspect of belonging, but it's a pipe-dreamy offering to our nest egg, as preposterous as deciding I'll be an Olympic luger. I want to stand tall in my own shoes but my role today is to sit and listen and shop and cook and feed and love and nuzzle and laugh. Dear wife, I got pushed in the pool and my toe bent back so I was up there with a nude woman. And with another chance to tell you nothing, I'd probably keep quiet because I'm definitely feeling the repercussions of a crime I did not commit. I'm guilty. Of seeing her nude in the mirror and not darting from the room. Of letting her kiss me, of leading her on. I can't recall my mindset. A resurgence of an old reaction to girls I kissed before we met. It had to do with a private wish. That I could absorb this woman without a drop of guilt. But of course, this was not to be. Because Freud said all you need to survive life is to love and to work. *Love*, the most tiredly trite word in the English language, but the only way to describe the vastness. Look at me for one second. Just give me your eyes, the time it takes to draw a breath.

I walk back upstairs. My wife and Katrina are sound asleep. I get in next to Jackie and lie silently. The rain is hard against the roof. The Appian River will form in the street and I still don't have sandbags. I will dream of a flood.

Moses and the Cookies

SATURDAY | *Hurricane Wilma arrives*

I wake to the storm. Both Jackie and Katrina are gone. From the staircase I can see the Appian River, deeper than ever. My lawn is underwater, all the way up to the hedges that line our front porch. I flip on the TV to see how bad it is. My new neighbors are back to unloading their truck. The downpour blows their boxes sideways as they come down the ramp. The daughters are helping, the older one in polka-dotted rain boots and a matching umbrella.

I pull my shoes on and step out into the mess. From my porch, I yell to my neighbors, "Hey, hi, not the best Floridian welcome in the world."

The father, bundled to the top of his head, can't hear me. He puts his hand by his ear. "What?"

"You'll need sandbags!"

He can't hear me.

"It might come up your front walkway!"

It's useless. We're separated by a river.

"I'll tell him," Alex says. I turn around and he's standing behind me, dressed in a yellow raincoat, holding a tray of cookies under tinfoil. He walks down the path into the river without the slightest hesitation. In a moment he's knee-deep in brackish rain-water, not to mention the downpour. The family can't believe their eyes, a tall and handsome delivery boy, stepping from the depths of our street to hand them something warm and sugary. Welcome to our crazy world. He talks with them, his back to me. He hands the tray to the oldest daughter and they exchange words. As he walks back, he laughs at the water just below his knees. He passes me on the porch. "Her name is Carlie. She could use a ride to school Monday."

I watch him walk back into the house, the door close. I wave to the family and they wave back.

My brain wants to celebrate. The medication is working. There's a sense the worst is over. He's a growing man, a friend even, some-one I love so much. I find Jackie in the kitchen and tell her what I saw. She follows me to the front porch and I point to the spot he walked into the water. Katrina and Tara run in the front hall to join us. "He did it already?"

I nod. "Your brother gave them the cookies."

"I wanted to do it."

My wife's phone rings.

"Hello? . . . Yes, this is she . . . Katrina Nicholson—yes?"

"Who is it?" I ask.

My wife's head slowly lowers and her fingers are now rubbing the bridge of her nose, straight between her eyes. "I understand," she says.

"Who is it?" I ask again.

My wife holds her open palm to me. Her eyes tear up fast.

"What?"

"Okay, I will," she says. "Thank you."

"Tell me," I say, when she hangs up.

"It's over," she says.

"What?"

"Lizzie wants her back," my wife says. "Lizzie wants her back."

Lovebugs

Lovebugs, *Plecia nearctica*. They're also known as honeymoon
flies, kissing bugs, and double-headed bugs. I'd say there's
eighty million on my patio right now.

"They call 'em that because they're always connected," I say.
"Look, it's like one bug with two heads. They never let go."

Katrina points at some in the pool. "They swim?"

"Iced drinks," my daughter says. "Come and get it."

Two lovebugs drop from somewhere and land on my ankle.

My wife sits up and brushes them off of me.

My son and daughter and Katrina all play Marco Polo. Jackie
reads off job possibilities for both of us. A job in San Francisco
perfect for her skill set. A CEO position in Silicon Valley. I take
notes for an essay I'm finishing for the *Huffington Post*. They like
my theme, the daddy diaries, essays from the perspective of a stay-
at-home dad, the newest sociological phenomenon sweeping the
nation. They may or may not publish it online.

The lawyers are calling our arrangement *interim foster care.* It means her parents can call and retrieve her at any time. But for now she's enrolled at school with my kids and is living as one of us. Lizzie is expected to leave a rehabilitation center in Cherry Hill, New Jersey, next week. I cannot say I wish Ray or Lizzie would take her home. I believe this is her home. But I've been wrong before. Ray stopped the threats. He calls rarely and usually promises Katrina gifts he never buys. I worry Lizzie will be calling soon and demanding we send her daughter home to her. If it happens, we'll have to do what she says, immediately, since her obligation to the court was fulfilled.

"There's a job for a chief digital officer in Berkeley," my wife says. "I'm calling the headhunter."

Katrina runs outside. "Phone call!" she says and hands me my cell.

"Hello?" I say.

"Good afternoon. This is Dr. Jacobs office."

"Who is it?" Jackie says.

"We have an opening for tomorrow at nine in the morning."

"Tomorrow?" I say.

"Yes, does that work for you?"

"Is it Lizzie's lawyer?" she asks.

"Yes," I say. "With Dr. Jacobs?"

"That's correct."

I look back at my wife.

"Okay. I can do tomorrow."

"Terrific," the woman says. "Please shave your pubic hair and ingest nothing but water before the surgery."

Silence.

"Hello?" she says.

"Yes. Yes, I'm here. I heard you," I say. "I'll see you tomorrow."

🙞　🙞　🙞

I am feeling a real fear that my testicles will never be the same. They've been this way since birth. Now I have to muck with them? In the waiting room my wife and I joke about running out of there and fucking in a nearby hotel. Ya know, for kid number three. As we wait to be called I think about my wife's words: "I feel like someone's missing from our dinner table."

"It's the right move," she says softly, convincing herself.

On the wall are some horrifying paintings. Depressing. The largest is a frontier landscape. A family attempts to pull their chuck wagon out of a mud pit while buffalo graze nearby. The wagon wheel is buried deep in the wet dirt. I think of castration, the moan of the slaughter. The vasa deferentia will be clipped to cut off the sperm and their Wild West mentalities. I think I smell ether. My penis is the size of a Tic Tac right now. I'm scared. But it's still the right choice. I think of the smell of Diaper Genie refills. Crying, shitting, whining, drooling, pissing.

A nurse with huge shoulders and no top lip is standing in the doorway. She says my name and I'm up, following her to the dungeon. I'm off to get hacked, my manhood in trouble. I try to get on top of the ridiculousness of it all. The doctor comes in. He's fat and I smell cigarettes.

"Done a ton of these," he says, open to any humor I might need to lighten the mood. I try a lame one, something about the amount of sleep he got the night before. The doctor laughs exactly the way he does for all of the suckers who come in here.

The nurse is a different person, not the lady from the waiting room. She is staring at my balls, my horrified turtle head. I get the needle to the scrotum, a deep pinch, then the flow of hot fluid in my groin, my inner thighs. This is going to hurt so much.

Another nurse walks in the room. "Your wife would like to speak to you."

The doctor steps back. "It's not a great time," he says.

"She says it's important."

"Okay," he says and places the silver tool in his hand on a tray. "Bring her in."

She steps into the room, holding back tears.

"What?" I say. "Tell me."

She looks like a little girl. So tough, with all that drive. I stand from the table and hold her.

"Can we go home?" she says in my ear. "I think we should go home."

Good-Bye

TUESDAY | *Sunny, mild winds off the gulf*

My daughter's bedroom door has a poster of a unicorn on it. Only his horn and tail are purple. Next to it is a poster of a panda holding a basketball. From inside the room comes the sound of two girls playing. I hear:

"You can't have a baby here."

"But I have to. My stomach is huge."

"Fine, I'll get the blankets."

"Wait, get my husband, I need him."

My phone call with Lizzie lasted an hour. She is indeed wrung out and currently dry. Her sentences were thoughtful, her tone laced with calm. She told me she thought I was the only friend of Ray's that gave her a chance. I told her I loved Katrina, and that I'd need to see her as she grew up.

I knock lightly, and the girls' dialogue ceases.

My daughter opens the door a crack. "We're busy, Daddy."

"Oh, sorry. I have to talk to you, though."

"What about?"

I step in and sit on the end of her bed. Katrina has a pillow under her shirt, making her belly "pregnant." She smiles at me as she removes it. "I was pretending I was having a baby."

"Let us play, Dad."

"Oh, I just wanted to talk to you guys about Katrina's mommy."

"Okay," my daughter says.

"Is that okay, Katrina? If we discuss your mom."

She nods and lies down on her bed.

"Lizzie got sick, you know that. But the good news is that she's better now and most importantly is ready to be a great and awesome mom."

"Is Katrina leaving us?"

I don't move my head, as they both face me.

"Yes."

My daughter's chin wrinkles. Her eyes blink as her head jets forward. "Why?" she says, and runs out of the room. Katrina stays still, a statue of herself, perhaps envisioning her life with her mother.

"She sounds great," I say. "Happy and like a different person. I think it's worth talking about what it might be like for you . . . if you went back to New Jersey for a while and . . . see what life might be like with your mom."

"I hate the idea," my daughter says from the hallway. "Hate it!"

Katrina looks down at her pillowcase, a design she picked out. Planets and stars.

"Can I take my bedding home?"

I nod. "Yes, you can. You can take all your things."

We sit in silence, and I just look at her. Her hair grew long here, a light red.

"Katrina?"

She faces me.

"I'll never stop loving you."

Her lips form a grin.

"You're a very special person to me. And if you ever need me . . . I'm just a phone call away."

A tear falls from her face and she wipes it as if it's a flea.

I stand and move to hold her.

"I love you, little girl," I say.

"I love you too."

⋈   ⋈   ⋈

Lizzie is at Newark Airport when we arrive. She has auburn hair now and a new smile and white jeans. Her eyes have focus. She hugs Katrina for a full two minutes. She then hugs me. I walk with them to the garage, even though I can tell Lizzie wants me to go. I talk about the flight, about sending more of her things next week. I'll need an address so I can ship her bedding and clothes.

"She has all that with me now."

"Okay, then," I say, my stomach pummeled with it all. "Call me soon. Okay? You have my number?"

Katrina nods and Lizzie leans over her to put her seat belt on.

"She knows how to put her own seat belt on," I say, and then regret it.

Lizzie faces me. "It's broken, okay? I need to do it. Thanks again for everything," she says.

I step back, and turn to leave. Lizzie is trying with all of herself to click that seat belt in. I get to the airport doors and look back.

Now she's slamming the passenger door closed but it keeps bouncing open. The seat belt is hanging out.

"The seat belt, Lizzie! See it? It's the seat belt."

She finally pulls the strap in the car and slams the door. It closes. I try to see Katrina but I can't. The reflection, the tint of the glass. I cannot see her. And then she's gone.

San Francisco

The fish tank selection my daughter and I find at PetSmart is vast. We decide to go a little bigger this time and get a castle, a treasure chest that opens, and living greens for nibbling. Meatball did not survive the move but it can't be said I didn't try. Still mourning, my daughter points to new friends, one striped, one purple, three orange.

At home, it takes us an hour or so to get it all hooked up. The two of us sit on the end of her bed and this time she's tall enough to feed them herself. The food sinks as the fish chase it, test it, take some into the castle.

"It's like we never left," she says.

There's a coffee shop right around the corner from our new place in Cole Valley. I sit there alone for the moment, my new notebook open to a blank page. I write #80 on the cover and draw a primitive sketch of the Golden Gate Bridge.

My son is still outside with a girl he met yesterday at his high school orientation. I watch him talk to her, touch her shoulder. When they walk inside, a pigeon flutters in the door and a tiny barista with a ponytail chases it out with a broom handle. I write *A pelican is not a pigeon* in notebook #80. It's surreal to be here, suddenly plucked from the summer's dream that was St. Petersburg. Alex's voice has deepened and turned slightly lispy, with Invisalign braces molded to his teeth.

"What can I get you?" he says to Samantha.

"Coffee with room," she says to my son. His girl drinks coffee. He asks me if I want anything. Who is this person? Buying a round? I didn't know he had a wallet. He counts his cash. I see too many singles.

"I'll take a Mexican Coke," I say, and he smiles at me while counting his money. This order is going to wipe him out but he's showing this woman how he rolls. I reap something visceral from it. It's a rush. Perhaps a reassurance that my inevitable aging and demise might come with a lesson.

"What's the notebook for?" says Samantha.

"Oh. I write."

"Cool. What do you write?"

The question hasn't come up in a while. I look down at the words I've just written.

"Will you read it?" she asks, this coffee-drinking fourteen-year-old in a violet beret.

"Okay," I say. I pull my chair closer to the table. "Back in Nor-Cal. A baby with no name will join us in the fall, a second girl. Jackie is officially independent, gathering up companies that need slick mobile and digital solutions. The other day the NFL called her, then UNICEF. Things may just work out for her. I'm writing a piece that may get rejected. Gotta swing to hit anything. It's a collection of essays about fatherhood in an era of redefined marital roles. I hear authors are selling their own work online without agents or even publishers. The times are a-changing. Another thought: an essay called 'Ginger's Mom.' It's about a mistake I almost made while digging myself out of a . . ."

I stop reading and look up at Samantha. She darts her head forward. "Out of a what? Digging yourself out of a what?"

"Dad?" my son says behind me. "I need three dollars."

I walk over and hand the cashier some money. My son's relieved. He places his cash back in his pocket. "Thanks."

"Here you go," he says, serving Samantha.

She thanks him and heads to put milk in her coffee.

"Dad?"

"Yes?"

"You were right." He opens my Coke for me and then his.

"About what, buddy?"

"I think this might be okay here. I like the feeling. San Francisco. Less sun, maybe . . . but more . . . substance. You know what I mean?"

I look at my boy across from me.

"Your change," the barista says to Alex. I stand, take the coins from her, and plop them in the tip jar. When I turn around my son is kissing Samantha, his hands on each of her shoulders. I wait a beat and head back to them, pretending I saw nothing. I open #80, a notebook so new it crackles. My pen touches the paper. *Alex. First kiss.* My phone chirps. It's a text from Jackie.

Tara has locked her door and won't come out of her room.

I text back. *Why?*

Alex's head tilts. He laughs. "Wanna try it?" he says. "It's the syrupy kind. A connoisseur's dream."

Samantha shakes her head. "Coffee for now," she says.

Jackie's text: *She says she's depressed.*

My eyes close on their own.

"You okay, Dad?" Alex says.

I smile at him and lean over #80. I write the words *Here we go again.* And then take a sip of my Coke.

Acknowledgments

I want to thank Jill Braff, my partner in life and work. I love you. Thank you to my supportive friends, who all happen to be great dads: Jon Levine, Steven Krasner, Jeff Schaffer, Matt Frank, Adam Titelbaum, Michael Black, David Hyman, Tom Riley, Matthew Schulte, Michael Hemsey, Dean Rubinson, and Terry Davenport. Thank you also to Judy Sternlight, Anne Horowitz, Mauna Eichner, Lee Fukui, Gretchen Koss, Meg Walker, David Walker, Siggy Rubinson, Lisa Davenport, Carol and Stephen Schulte, Kathleen Caldwell, Michael Sippey, Lily Howard, Esther Happle, and Lynn Carey. I'm very grateful to my family, Henry Braff, Ella Braff, Anne and David Brodzinsky, Hal and Elaine Braff, Zach Braff, Adam Braff, Shoshi Braff, Lara Brodzinsky, Michelle Moder, Lila Braff, Blaze Braff, Jagger Braff, Jessica Kirson, Jennifer Gelman, and Milo Braff, my goldendoodle, who sat next to me for the entire journey.

About the Author

Joshua Braff was raised in New Jersey and now lives in Lafayette, California with his wife and two children. He is a graduate of the Saint Mary's College MFA program and is the author of the novels, *The Unthinkable Thoughts of Jacob Green* and *Peep Show*. Visit www.joshuabraff.com for more information.

CPSIA information can be obtained at www.ICGtesting.com
Printed in the USA
LVOW11s1625160615

442681LV00007B/987/P